(C) DAN BROTHERS 2022

PROLOGUE

You've all heard the legend of Dr Jekyll and Mr Hyde. The frightening monster who drags Dr Jekyll into the flames. What if all was not as it seemed?

This is the story of a man who has no escape. He has no identity or purpose. He is kept as a mental and physical prisoner while his alter ego continued his life as normally as he could. There's only so long someone can keep such a secret.

Can they work together in their most desperate times of need?

CHAPTER ONE

MEET MR HYDE

The cellar lies shrouded in darkness and dampness, a dim light in the corner casting eerie shadows across the room. Among the clutter of lab equipment and towering stacks of books, a figure slumps in a chair. The air is thick with the pungent mix of body odour and dampness, an unpleasant odour that clings to your senses. A feeble stream of light seeps in through a frosted window, revealing the solitary figure.

This figure is closely watched and meticulously observed—it's the duty of Doctor Jennifer Carmichael. A specialist who thrives on complex matters, she keeps a clinical distance. The man in the chair begins to stir, his head inching closer to the feeble light source, casting eerie shadows that outline his silhouette. There's no struggle or escape attempt; it's gone beyond that, and he's resigned to this grim reality.

The man wears a soiled white shirt with a loosely tied black tie, reminiscent of how Dr. Jekyll would always loosen his tie and roll up his sleeves before sleep. As his senses start to awaken, he utters in a deep, gravelly voice.
"I can smell you. Who are you?" He says in a deep gravelly voice. Dr Carmichael remains sat in the chair motionless, around twelve foot away, with her notepad now closed on her lap. Dressed in a smart suit and doused some nice perfume, her hair tied back neatly and wearing her reading glasses. Far too well dressed to be sat in a damp and mouldy cellar she thought to herself.

Her handbag rested quietly by her side on the cold concrete floor. "Another doctor summoned to our rescue, no doubt?" Hyde's tone dripped with sarcasm as he continued to speak. She remained still and silent, well aware of Hyde's cunning nature, thanks to the insights Dr. Jekyll had shared with her.
"I wish you would liberate me from this living nightmare," he implored, his words deliberate and purposeful.
"That's rather curious. I was told that you were the source of the problem," the doctor finally addressed

Hyde, breaking her silence. Her demeanour was one of nervous anticipation, but not fear. She had navigated treacherous waters before, having witnessed her father's abuse of her mother during her formative years and enduring abusive relationships in her university days. This man didn't unnerve her, especially since Jekyll had assured her of his inability to escape.

"ME? I am the very reason we draw breath! Yet he incarcerates me like a prisoner, night after night!" Hyde's agitation grew evident as he strained against his restraints. "And I am the issue? Ha! He hides behind the façade of a doctor—nothing more than a kidnapper and a wretched drunk." Hyde's voice echoed through the room, his body leaning forward in the chair, anchored firmly to the floor.

The restraints are holding his force, but only because they are so well re-enforced. He knows it will make him look worse the angrier he gets but he just cant help himself. "You seem upset with Dr Jekyll." The doctor probing him for information.

"Come closer, so I can see you? Your perfume is pungent. Your voice is tepid. I want to see that face of yours."
"Then we can talk properly?" The doctor asks of him.
"You come close and I will tell you anything you want to know." Hyde promises. She gently and slowly stands up and moves he chair into a better lit part of the room. It scrapes along the uneven floor of the basement as she moves gracefully, light on her feet as if she studied ballet or gymnastics to a high level. She sits back down so her face is now in full light.

Her light blonde hair slicked back in a ponytail and a notepad back resting on her lap. She doesn't appear to have started writing.
"Happy?" She asks.
"Ecstatic." He reacts in his typically sarcastic manner. "You said I seem upset. Let me explain what happens here night after night. Then you might see why I *seem* upset." He goes on. He stops to take a moment to compose himself and look around. "I wake up, tied to this contraption. It's a voice-activated lock that only responds to a certain phrase, from a certain voice, which only a certain good doctor knows. I don't get to eat, I don't get to drink. I don't get to walk around, I don't get to express myself in any way shape or form

while he lives his life guilt free playing the good and philanthropic doctor" He pauses for a second and the doctor interrupts. "How does…"

"DO NOT INTERRUPT ME!" Hyde yells for the first time in her presence, straining every part of his shackles as if he was a dog on a lead trying to attack someone trespassing on his turf. Carmichael is visibly shaken and moves her chair back an inch or two as if to show him that she's physically not happy with the shouting. Like when you train a puppy, it has to know its done bad. "I apologise. You just, you asked me to explain - and then interrupt - it's extremely frustrating." Hyde offers the apology as the doctor remains quiet. "This barbaric man has made me like this. What else do you call a man who does this? Your capture? Your kidnapper, your boss? He is a power-hungry freak. How can he get away with this for so long? We used to be friends? We used to be inseparable? What has he done to us?" Hyde becomes almost emotional at the thought.

The doctor pauses for long enough to make sure she doesn't get scolded again. "What do you mean you used to be inseparable?" she says after his pause.

"I mean we were always getting out of scrapes together. He used to get himself in all sorts of trouble. I would be the one to help get us out of it. He didn't lock me up when he needed me then, did he?" he seemed to flit from anger to fond memories. Maybe those memories made the anger worse, knowing how things used to be.

"So you feel like he used you?" The doctor asks.
"Don't do that." Hyde politely requests.
"Don't do what?"
"Talk to me like one of your patients. That's not what I am. You are not here to study me. I am not the issue here. The good Doctor has called you here to help him resolve HIS issues. I am fine with how things used to be." He has been so frustrated by the amount of invasions he has been subject to over the years.
"You keep talking about the ways things used to be. Tell me about how it used to be." She asks as she opens the notebook for the first time.
"There was a time when the good doctor loved to get into a scrape or two - he knew I would rescue him. We were twelve years old and walking through a crowd" Hyde reminisced.

He starts telling a story of when they were at school. Jekyll went to a nice comprehensive school, where he learnt to be studious and focussed, but it didn't come without problems. The school was busy and there were always people out to make sure they are top dog in the school. Older kids would often knock the smaller kids about just to show them that they are the ones to look out for. These bigger kids walking through a crowd and gives a shove into a young Jekyll. Jekyll wasn't a push over but he also wasn't a big tough kid. His strength came from Hyde, but because of that he would never back down, so he shoves them back and it becomes incredibly obvious it's going to turn sour. "You need to watch where you're going little man" the big kid squares up to Jekyll. He is almost 6 foot tall and not far off that wide, Jekyll was not intimidated. Hyde would simply wait in the wings until needed.
"Is that so?" Jekyll laughs at him.
"Don't you talk back to me, you'd wish you hadn't."
The kid wasn't used to people talking back to him. Especially pip squeaks like this one.
"I already wish I hadn't. Your conversation is boring me to death." Jekyll had a smart mouth and used it on a

regular basis when he was a kid. It often landed them both in trouble.

"Right, that's it..." The kid grabs Jekyll and punches him in the gut, he crumples to the floor in a heap. The kid and his mates surround him cheering and laying the odd kick in on him. As the noise starts to dissipate they can hear Jekyll laughing...but it was no longer Jekyll. Hyde grabs one of the boy's feet, smashes his elbow into his knee making it go backwards, it makes a horrible cracking sound as he does, the noise is almost drowned out by the kids high pitched squeal as he crumples to the floor. As Hyde rises, he head butts one of the other kids out cold - now its just him and the big kid. "Bullies. You're all the same. Cowards." Hyde faces up and looks at him with pure evil in his eyes. The kid was in a state of tears and panic seeing his pals crippled by this kid almost half his size. "Listen - I er..." is about all he manages before he turns and runs. Hyde gives chase for a short while and jumps on his back sending him crashing into a heap on the floor. Hyde bites his ear off and the big kid screams in agony. Grinning a bloody grin, he grabs the ear from his still clenched teeth and smears it all in his face so

he's covered in his own blood. The kid is frozen by panic and his tears pinning him
 to the floor in a state of shock and fear.
"You're lucky he doesn't he like to kill people - or you'd be dead in a heartbeat." Hyde whispers in his good ear before wiping his mouth and hands on the big kids coat before standing up and straightening himself up and walked off casually leaving the boy writhing on the floor holding his ear in one fans and the bloodied wound in the other.

"That's pretty horrific for a young kid to see and be a part of ." The doctor observes and points out the obvious having heard the story that Hyde has probably told to many therapists over the years. She has learnt that in cases like this, patients try and put people off as soon as possible. She was busy making copious amounts of notes, about the story Hyde assumed. " I assumed someone of your position would disapprove. You come from a different world. We will literally do anything to protect one another." Hyde tells her in no uncertain terms, starting to get agitated. You can see it in his disposition, he looks less comfortable than he did before. I guess anyone would be too if they were tied to a chair all night every night. "So why did it go wrong?" The doctor probed further.

"Now that is a story. I'm not sure we have time - and I certainly don't want to go through it while I am chained up like an animal" Hyde's entire demeanour seems to have changed. More withdrawn.

"You're always chained up like this?"

"Yes. He doesn't like me on the loose. I am sure there is another way to get out of these shackles come morning time, in case the voice activation fails."

"He must have a back up key somewhere close by."

"I guess. I have searched everywhere… well, as much as I can with these restraints on. Maybe you can…"

"I'm not here to help you escape Mr. Hyde." She interrupts him and stops him dead in his tracks regaining some control and composure over the situation.

"Then you're happy to be an accomplice to this kidnapping?" Hyde asks her, trying to tug on her heartstrings.

"Kidnapping?" Puzzled, the doctor really starting to get to the bottom of his real feelings.

"What else do you call it? A man, held, chained against his will night after night?"

"Protection maybe? For you, him, and others?" She tries to comfort him and she see he is spiralling.
"Easy excuses. The longer I spend here the more I yearn for freedom. To express myself."
"So, if you were to be released right now what would you do?" asks the doctor, really trying to get under the surface of it all.
Hyde pauses and closes his eyes for a couple of seconds. "Come closer and I'll whisper it." He says in a more sinister sounding voice. He didn't mean for it to sound sinister, he just wasn't used to having company nowadays. He reacted in a way which he didn't intent to a lot of the time.
"Mr. Hyde, really I…" She begins before Hyde interrupts her. "You want to know what I want… come close. I won't bite you. I'm not an animal despite what he might tell you." Hyde spoke in a softer voice, a little more friendly this time. Staring at her with his big blue eyes. Looking straight into her soul. The doctor, for the first time is losing a little composure.

She takes a big gulp and an uncomfortable shuffle as she straightens herself out and walks over with her chair. She purposely places it next to Hyde, perhaps closer than you'd expect her to given the circumstances. "Is this what you wanted?" she asks politely again. Hyde makes a satisfying humming noise. Takes a deep sniff of her. "Do you know it's been such a long time since I have had company here. Thank you so much for coming."

"As I have said, I am not here for you Mr. Hyde. Doctor Jekyll asked me to come." She pauses for a couple of beats of her heart, she felt it might beat so hard that Mr Hyde might hear it. Hyde just grins at her "When was the last time you were set free?"

"You mean the last time I escaped? He doesn't set me free. He doesn't like me wandering the streets." he looks out of the small window as if to plead for someone to drag him out of it "He says I will get us in trouble."

"How did you escape? Where did you go? What did you do?" She seems excited by the thought that he got away for a while.

"I managed to untie the ropes he used to use. That's why he now uses keys and voice-activated systems. I got free of the ropes and escaped. I went and got myself in a little trouble. Until recently of course I haven't been able to come out to play at all. It's a serum you see? He creates it, it suppresses me apparently." Hyde explains.

"So, why stop taking the serum" She quizzes Hyde.

"He hasn't, he's simply growing a tolerance to it. Which means I am growing a tolerance to it." He continues to explain.

"So, what happened when you escaped?" The doctor referred to the earlier note she made.
"I'm not going to indulge you in these stories all night long Doctor. If you want me to give you more - then you have to help me out. Help me find a key or means of escape. I won't run, I won't fight. I just want a drink with some company."
"That's not going to happen Mr. Hyde" She closes her notebook and leans back in her chair.
"Then you might as well leave now. I am not telling you anything else why I am cooped up like an animal."
"Mr. Hyde, please." She pleads her case.
"No. Leave me." He instructs her.
She stands up and puts her note book in her bag and places her black overcoat on over her suit. She looks at him and reflects on the conversation. "This really is a curious case. Goodbye Mr Hyde." She disappears into the shadows and he can only hear her leave through the basement door. He closes his eyes.

The morning sun basks over the front of Dr Jekyll's house. Sun flooding the rooms to the front of the house. He lives in a very opulent area with the money he made from his years of doctoring before retiring to lead the life of relative recluse. Dr Carmichael and Dr Jekyll are sitting in his dining room talking. She felt a little strange speaking with a man who yesterday was a different man – at least in his own head. The dining room sat in the centre of his luxurious Georgian townhouse. An oak looking table in the middle with a single light over the top and fabric topped chairs around the outside. He kept the house very clean not like the basement where Mr Hyde spent most of the time. "So what did you make of your conversation with our friend?" Dr Jekyll asked whilst pouring the tea into a small china cup with a matching saucer.

"He is very upset. He seems like a scared individual. He's not of sound mind." The doctor stated her observations clearly and concisely so there was no confusion.
"No shit Doctor. He kills people that will given half the chance, that's why he has to stay there." Dr Jekyll responds as if it's the most ridiculous thing he's heard.

"Keeping him locked in there night after night is not a viable long-term solution." The doctor tells him her opinion.
"That's why I have you here. He seems to have grown a tolerance to the serum I have developed which keeps him at bay. I need you to help get rid of him for good." Jekyll getting easily agitated by the doctors willingness to be impartial.
"I am not sure what I can do for you" she said "You two need to develop trust. Keeping him locked up will not allow this to happen." She continued in a very calm and trusting voice.
"Oh you think I should let him out? Do you realise what would happen?" Jekyll said with a nervous laugh.
"Maybe if you laid out some ground rules he wouldn't cause any trouble. He knows there needs to be boundaries. He says you two used to be very close why can't you reconcile?" The doctor sensing Jekyll's mood.

"Those days are long gone. I can't forgive myself if somebody gets hurt because of him or me. Getting rid of him is the only option I can see." He says in a sad remorseful voice. He looks solemnly out of window onto his spacious driveway, remembering how times used to be.

After a short pause for observation she breaks the silence "I will see him again next week for you. But there has to be a better solution than this." as she sees a tear trickling down his nose and falling onto the table in front of him. She stands up and puts on her coat, picks up a bag walks towards the door and let herself out without so much of a word from either party.

CHAPTER TWO

THE VILLAIN

Tony is a big chap in personality and stature. He and his henchmen run a lot of the drug syndicate in the city. The relationship he has with Jinny Wu is a good one that benefits them both, but doesn't involve drugs, it involved something much more sinister and valuable, children. He find buyers from abroad for the merchandise and she supply's them. He's a middle man who makes money from exploiting the children. He and his thugs Freddie and Tommy were usually by his side and they hung out in their local pub. They used the Honeycoombe as their base. People knew to give them a wide birth when they came in which suited everyone. Freddie was a tall muscly man who was an expert in kick-boxing and MMA. Jonny was shorter but wider, with plenty of battle scars from his days of football hooliganism. Tony was much more clean cut and always dressed sharply.

The pub felt like a typically British pub in the countryside. Oak tables, roaring fire, flowery curtains with matching pelmets. Tony and his crew were occupying a table in the far corner where they could talk about their unscrupulous behaviour in peace and quiet. They were in the pub discussing the deal they are going to make with Jinny when Deano sheepishly comes to the table.
"Alright Deano?" Tony belts out in his broad welsh accent.
Deano was a scrawny little drug runner for the boys and has helped them make money of the years. But the truth is, plenty of people would be able to do the same job, so people like Deano become disposable in Tony's world. "Tony, hello mate, can we have a chat?" He asks still struggling to bring his hands out of his pockets.
"Of course mate, grab a seat"
"In private if we can?"
"We're all mates here Deano my old fruit!" Tony assured him as Freddie stands up and pulls a chair out for him. "Here you are pal, have this seat." He offers with a sinister smile. Deano felt like his was well and truly in the lions den. He nervously sat down as he was told to and started the speech he rehearsed plenty of times in the car park before this meeting.

"It's er, it's about the er, money I owe ya" he manages to bundle out nothing like he had rehearsed, watching the psychotic 6'4 Freddie over his shoulder.
"You don't have it?" Tony guesses.
"No, no I don't."
"That's ok Deano, you've still got 24 hours" he tells him in a rather chipper tone.
"Tony that's not enough time man." With that he feels one of Freddie's paws grab him by his ear and smash his head into the table. He leans over him closely and whispers in his ear "listen you little sausage…"
Tony interjects "That's enough. Deano, you're a resourceful little geezer" mocking his cockney accent "you'll find a way" and with that Freddie allows him back up and sees him out. Tommy watched the whole thing with a wry smile drinking his pint. It takes a lot to disturb that man from his pint. Deano rubs his ear now bright red and straightens himself out. He stands up and looks at the men individually before taking his leave.
"Come on boss, we have to and meet Jinny at her casino." Freddie looks at his watch as he straightens the table out.

"Tommy, you stay here incase that little weasel comes back yeah" Tony knew he'd prefer to stay where it's quiet and there's beer.

They leave the pub and enter the casino. It was down the back alley behind an estate agents behind a little metal door, you wouldn't know it was there. Seems to be the same faces in the same places but Tony liked that, he doesn't like surprises. He and Freddie sit at a table and have a drink after putting some money down. Freddie would always drink water and Tony usually a neat whiskey. The waitress knew their orders by heart. They played some Roulette and sipped their brinks, just killing time until Jinny came to see them.
"You think they can do the job? Freddie asked referring to the people they are smuggling in.
"Who gives a fuck? No one knows they're here, if they can we'll just…"
"What? Do them in?"
Tony shrugs in an agreeable manner as Jinny Wu approaches.
"Hello lads" she welcomed them in a friendly tone.
"Tony, have you put weight on? You need to get down the gym with this one!" She refers to Freddie squeezing his shoulder.

"Ah thanks very much. You're looking radiant as ever." Rather bashfully and embarrassed in-front of Freddie. "We have another shipment coming in next week Tony, I assume the buyer is still on board." Jinny asks in a matter of fact manner.
"He's raring to go, just got the containers cleaned out. Filthy bastards shit everywhere." He reassures Jinny that he's ready.
"Animals Tony. Thank god for people like you eh?" She strokes his arm as she compliments him. She passes an envelope over to Freddie and gives him a little wink. "Anyway, I have to be off boys" she excuses herself and disappears onto the casino floor.

They finish their drinks and leave the casino. They continue to an old office block building which looks derelict and has been for some years. It was around ten floors high with windows broken or graffiti covered.
They head in through an old creaky door and wonder down the dimly lit stairs into the basement. As they approached the end of the stairs they could hear talking and machinery going. They enter the door and there was Tony's empire laid out in front of him. Piles of cocaine and pills bagged up in different sizes and

quantities ready to go. Right from 2kg packages to small single use bags- a team of people were preparing it all. To the right there was a big bundle of counted cash ready to be laundered. It was a slick operation and he did very little to disrupt it unless he had to. Freddie and Tony went into the office at the other end of the room and sat down on the sofas.

"You think our friend Deano will get the cash?" Freddie asks him looking out of the door onto the room of drugs and cash.
"Don't matter. He's a dead man walking either way." Tony tells him.
Freddie shrugged his shoulders and looked to the desk where there is a full decanter of scotch. "Fancy a glass?" He asked Tony.
"Thought you'd never bloody ask." He quips back quickly.

Tony was a small time crook back in the day. His family were wealthy enough and his parents were far too busy buying and selling businesses to notice what young Tony did or didn't get up to. They paid for martial arts classes and given that he came from an upstanding background he very much knew how to talk to people (and usually get his own way). He moved away from Wales when he was in his late teens and immediately fell in love with the city life. Getting into the wrong crowds almost immediately, he starting running drugs, dealing drugs and money laundering. It all escalated in a row with the boss and Tony ended up killing the boss and everyone turned to him for leadership. To be that position by your early 20's was pretty daunting but he's got used to it over time. He was soon one of the most feared criminals in the city with a network to rival any other gang.

CHAPTER THREE

BAD HABITS

Like children, over protective, super strength alter egos need routine. They are creatures of habit. So, Dr Jekyll made sure that him and Mr Hyde had just that. Unfortunately, for Mr Hyde, that routine almost always resulted in being chained up in a basement, with no hope of getting away or no hope of mental or physical stimulus. Jekyll would awake from his slumber and escape the shackles of the night before, go upstairs and have a couple of coffees before heading for a shower (or on a rare occasion a bath.) He had hoped that the longer he spent in the shower, Hyde might simply wash away. No such luck. Jekyll liked to keep respectable, so he would spend time pruning himself after his shower. Nose hairs, ear hairs, eyebrows and of course making sure he was clean shaven. He would spend such a long time looking in the steam covered mirror trying to make sure Mr Hyde was well covered. Being presentable was a very important lesson he learnt from his dad. If you want to be a respected member of society you must be presentable. He remembered this very clearly drummed into him from his father. No such advice was given on how to deal with an out of control maniacal split personality, but still, you can't have everything, can you now?

After pruning himself, he would go to his very dull coloured wardrobe and choose a very boring shirt to go with his well fitted suits. He always wore a suit, he didn't really know why anymore, but he did, almost every day. He liked the idea of being seen to be a pillar of the community but in truth he doesn't do that much any more for the community but still get invited to fund raisers and networking events which he seldom attends. He then goes and has some breakfast. Usually, porridge or toast. Jekyll then always goes to the local corner shop to get the papers, and more often than not a bottle of whiskey. The journey would talk him on a lovely scenic walk through the park and past the lake. He would often watch people out with their kids feeding the ducks, knowing he would probably never be able to settle down. Three is crowd as they say.

The shop was only six minutes walk from his house, a small shop with the essentials. He knew the shop keeper Sam quite well. Sam was a short Eastern European chap with a big thick glasses and an even bigger zest for life. He loves colourful jumpers and always tries to make Dr Jekyll smile. Jekyll walks up to the counter with his whiskey and papers. "Morning doctor, had another late night?"
"You could say that. An acquaintance had me up all night" Jekyll told Sam as he scanned the papers through the machine.
"These late nights will be the death of you doctor, can I get you anything else?
"Papers and whiskey Sam, always papers and whiskey" retorted the Dr.
"You never buy your cigarettes from here doctor?" he asks Dr Jekyll, knowing he smokes on a semi regular basis.
"You know I get imports...cheaper my dear friend" Jekyll packs the stuff into a little blue plastic bag. Jekyll uses his phone to pay contactless and walks off "Thanks, Sam, I'll see you later" He tells him as he heads to the door..

"Hope to see you tonight then doctor" Sam shouts as he leaves.

Jekyll waves over his shoulder without looking back as he leaves, I hope not he thinks to himself as he makes his way home. Night time visits are not his routine, therefore must be Mr Hyde.

Often he will have some social engagements with local colleges, museums, conferences etc, but he always makes sure before tea time. Dr Jekyll rarely ate lunch and was therefore ravenous at tea time. One of the triggers for Mr Hyde is being hungry. It makes him angry and want to hunt for his own food. Not that he gets the chance to, but Jekyll really notices the difference if he is hungry for sure. After dinner he settles down to read the papers and drink at least 1/3 of a bottle of his favourite whiskey. He has a small glass and a decanter, although at the rate he drinks, he may as well just drink from the bottle.

When he's had enough of the days shenanigans (usually around 9pm) he retires to the basement for his nightly routine. Dreaming up a password and puts his prompts on the board so he remembers the word come morning time. He injects his serum and throws three sleeping pills down his neck. Then he places himself in the voice activated shackles and holds the button so he can say the word of his choosing. The shackles tighten and he is set for the night. Dr Jekyll didn't like having such a regimented regime, it left very little wriggle room for fun or meeting people, but he felt it very necessary. He didn't want to risk Hyde causing trouble. Mr Hyde was a bit like a gremlin. You can't over feed it or get it over excited. The last time he managed to let Hyde escape he sank a boat that he thought was bringing drugs into the country. It may well have been the case but there was no evidence and the police would never buy the story. So he spent weeks trying to avoid the police and all related news stories. Turns out they were smuggling drugs and the police didn't investigate too vigorously. Somewhere within him Dr Jekyll knew that Hyde was trying to do good. But that was clouded with the destruction and devastation he caused.

The thing that Dr Jekyll could never get used to was that people would never know if its him or Mr Hyde. Surely they could spot one persons behaviour from another he would often think to himself. He has had plenty of chats with Mr Hyde over the years about how they can live in unison with each other. A symbiotic solution Dr Jekyll would call it. In their twenties, they had months of working like this, but inevitably it went wrong when Hyde attacked someone or Jekyll blamed him for his own actions - it depends who you ask. Dr Jekyll was known for a few bad habits. Drinking, gambling, womanising, maybe this is part of the real reason he keeps Jekyll locked up night after night. He blames the bad things on him his alter ego. Of course there are three versions of the story, Dr Jekyll's version, Mr Hyde's version, and then the truth.

Dr Jekyll is working in the basement. He is frantically searching for ingredients for his serum, the serum which Hyde is building immunity to, but it does keep him at bay for the majority of the time. He pulls out an old leather bound engraved book. It looks like something you would find on the wizards bookshelf. He carefully opens the pages and slowly flicks through them, as if he didn't want to cause any damage or even fingermarks. He stops at the page and scribbles some notes on a piece of paper next to the book. As usual with Dr Jekyll, he isn't organised and can't find a pen so ends up scribbling it down with a piece of flint and carving the writing into the paper. He very gently and very carefully closes the book and places it back into its rightful place. He treats it like most people would treat a newborn baby, fearful of any harm that may come to it. He takes out his mobile phone and enters a number that he has scribbled on an old piece of paper in his desk. He takes a deep breath before pushing the call button, as if to prepare himself. The phone rings four times before somebody at the other end answers.

"Miss Wu" he begins the conversation "I need some of your special ingredients."
"Dr Jekyll" she responds. "How nice to hear from you. We have missed you at the casino." Jinny Wu ran an underground Chinese Casino. It's the type of place people went when they didn't want to be seen by others, or they didn't have the correct means of funds to go to a normal casino. Lots of people owed Jinny Wu some money, at a hefty interest rate as you'd imagine and those that owe money for too long seem to go missing.
"That's kind of you Miss Wu" he responds in a polite but slightly rushed manner "I will come back again

soon I promise. But for now I need help with these ingredients. I cant think where else I can get them?" "What do you need?" Jinny seems to understands the urgency of the situation. She has dealt with Dr Jekyll and his requests before. She knows he's creating some kind of potion but doesn't tend to ask too many questions.

Again he takes a deep breath and mutters "Tiger's blood" reading from the notes he ripped into the page. "That's the only thing I don't have" Dr Jekyll was a very resourceful man.

The serum was created from a recipe dating back to the 1700's, designed to help people with split personality disorder. It's the closest thing Jekyll had found over the years that helps to keep Hyde at bay. "That's no problem Dr Jekyll, come to the casino the day after tomorrow." She hangs up and Dr Jekyll sits in his office chair. He didn't like going to the casino. Miss Wu was terrifying at the best of times. She was a slight woman in her 30's, always looking glamorous. Everyone suspected where her fortune came from but no one knew. She has long dark hair and always dressed in dark clothing.

After hanging up the phone she spends some time walking around her casino, schmoozing with the regulars and the not so regulars. She was the face of her business and proud of it. She meanders towards the back exit minded by two huge security guards and into a dimly lit back room.

A man is chained to a chair, beaten and bloodied. Balding and a very untidy beard, untidy clothes and some old dirty off white trainers. One of Jinny's thugs approaches her as she enters. "He doesn't have your money Miss Wu, but he is still in here gambling" he explains to her.
"That's very disappointing" Miss Wu says as she saunters toward the man chained to the chair. She walks around the chair as if to intimidate the beaten and bloodied man even more. "How much of the money can you pay back?" she asks him as she bends down and looks into his eyes.
"I don't have any of it, that's why I was here trying to earn it back" The man cried terrified.
"So you borrow money from me to gamble. Then you come into my casino and gamble some more and cheat - to be able to pay me back my money? You are in some hot water my friend." She relays the story to

him waltzing around the room, the man begins to sniffle even more. "Untie him ... please" she requests of her thugs. They oblige and stand him up. He can barely stand as two thugs hold him up.

"I'm sorry" he mumbles.
"How dare you cheat in my venue." she says as she pulls a small blade from a hidden holster behind her back under her jacket. Its gold with an ornate handle what she holds firmly as she pushes it against the mans skin. He can feel the cold blade piercing his skin and a small trickle of blood winds it's way down his neck and absorbs into his loose fitting T-shirt.
"Please" he begs as he feels the pressure of the blade on his skin pressing harder.
"I'd have to hear a really good excuse to not push this blade all the way into your trachea boy" she explains to him not breaking eye contact.
"Please," he's now crying, a literal mixture of blood, sweat and tears soaking into his clothes. "I have a family" he implores.
Wu looks disappointed in the answer. "It's too late for that" she says as she pushes the blade into the skin. Slowly looking him in the eyes as the blade penetrates deeper. He tries to struggle but the thugs are still

restraining him and the blood pours down his neck and all over his already bloodied shirt.

Jinny just watches, comfortably, the light goes out in his eyes as she wipes the blade of her knife on his shoulder, the only clean bit of his T-shirt. She places the knife back securely in its holster and turns to walk away. The thugs drop the body like a sack of spuds now its limp and lifeless, laying in a pool of his own blood.
"Get this cleaned up" she strides away being sure not to tread in any of the mess. The lads know the drill. They get to work immediately. She leaves the room from a different door she came in through which leads to the outside, grabbing a coat and securing the waist tie as she walks through. It's night time and raining just hard enough that she needed the coat.

The moonlight was shimmering through the light steaks of rain. The casino was located not too far from the docks. She could hear the rain drops bouncing on the metal of the containers as she walked among them. These docks were where most people suspected she brought her drugs in to the country, but again no one knew for sure. She was very secretive and kept her circle very small. She marched over towards a container with a man outside with a rifle. He was pointing the nozzle toward the floor, a short hair cut and wearing all black military style clothes. Obviously a military man. "All Ok?" she asked as she approached.

"All good Miss Wu" the man responded. She continues past the container, gets into her car and closes the door. She takes out some sanitiser from her glove box and gives her hands a clean. She looks in the mirror and makes sure her hair is in good order. She starts the car and puts on some of her favourite music and drives off in her dark estate car. She would often disappear like this without a word, but no one knew where to. Of course people has their ideas and there were many rumours but that was the extent of it.

Another night passes with Hyde restrained. Another night of frustration and loneliness for the so called captured beast. By the time we wakes, the sun has already subsided but he usually gets to see the sun come up. A rare moment of emotional levity for a sad and depressing way of life he is forced to endure. He couldn't help his thoughts moving towards the doctor. He couldn't help but wonder would the doctor come back for another chat. She seemed keen on him, or maybe thats just her way of getting the most out of their time together. Either way he would like to find out. He closes his eyes with a small streak of sunlight hitting his face, Hyde could deduce its probably the start of spring. He kept his eyes closed until he faded back into Dr Jekyll's subconscious. Dr Jekyll slowly awoke from his restless slumber. He always felt so tired, realistically sleeping two or three hours a night. He wouldn't bother at all it wasn't for Hyde needing to be subdued. He was used to no sleep by now, it became habit for him.

His wrists would always hurt from where Hyde would try and pull free from the restraints night and after night. He sometimes thought Hyde would go overboard on purpose to cause him extra aggravation in the morning. When Hyde used to roam free, Dr Jeykll would often wake up with scars, or aches and pains that he would only imagine where they came from. How long could this go on? Everyday there was a new password for the voice activated chains. It was written in code just within eyesight behind him so that he could be able to see it, but he was sure Hyde wouldn't be able to, and further still wouldn't be able to decipher. It was visible on the edge of a picture frame which acted as a mirror. It would have lots of words for whatever the code may be. Gorge, gullet etc.... "Oesophagus" he proclaimed to enable the voice activated lock to open and free himself. He pulls his hands round to the front of his body and rubs his aching wrists, stands up and straightens himself up. He takes a moment to clear up the basement and make sure it was ready for his inevitable visit later that night. He stumbles wearily up the stairs and turns on the coffee machine. He needs at least two coffees in the morning to function, especially if Hyde has been active and refusing to sleep.

As the coffee machine was whirring Jekyll's thoughts drifted back to Jinny and the serum he was developing. Keen to get it sorted once and for all. He snaps out of his thoughts as the coffee machine ends and he slams the first down the hatch and get the next one going. Slams some toast in the toaster and gets himself upstairs and out of his well worn clothes and gets in the shower. The water always started cold so he stands a meter back for the first 30 seconds before showering. Turning the heat up once he's in there to see how hot he could handle it. He dried himself off and got dressed. He again dressed smart - he was a doctor after all. No one was clear what he was a doctor of, but everyone knew he was a doctor. He was not practising anymore since a few alcohol induced incidents. By the time he left his house it was past lunch time. He often got concerned when he lost track of time - did Hyde come out for an hour or two? It was only the lack of chaos and destruction that made him think that couldn't be the case.

When he was in his early 20's Hyde would often visit for an hour or two and end up in a brothel or strip club. This was Jekylls side of the story at least, and boy is he sticking to it! He made his way to Jinny Wu's casino. The entrance was down an alleyway behind an estate agents, there was a steel door that was always open. You have to go through that door and then wait for another internal door to be answered. The door opened, they knew Dr Jekyll from years gone by.

He walks in amongst the smoke and degenerates at the casino tables drinking and laughing. The room was pretty big with gambling tables and machines surrounding them incase people want to gamble without the shame of the dealer looking them in the eye while they gambled away their children's inheritance. Half of these people Dr Jekyll would never associate with, the other half he wouldn't admit to associating with. He sits down at a table with two other people sat at it. He didn't even check what the games was, he was just passing the time, waiting for Jinny Wu to come and see him. She was always watching, he knew that. She was always watching from her office, the cameras were not obvious but he knew they were there. At some point she would come and see him. He needed that Tiger Blood. So he chucked down a few hundred and saw the game was blackjack. He liked blackjack. It wasn't a lucky game for him, but he liked it. He didn't want to spend too much time in there, he was only there to get the ingredients he needed, then he was gone! A tall lady in a short dress delivered a whiskey to him with ice in a short glass. She places the napkin on the table next to him and puts the drink down on top of it and walks off with nothing more than a smile. She didn't present a bill, everyone knew to pay their tab before they left Jinny Wu's place. Dr Jekyll sat and drank his drink, joining in with the occasional conversation with the croupier about the type of dog he had and how he loves to train it to do menial tricks for treats. After around an hour of drinking and gambling Jinny came into the room and placed a hand on his shoulder as if to leave him in no doubt that she was ready to have a chat with him.

He stands up and hurriedly shovels the chips he has in front of him into his pocket, not that he had trust issues but they were all degenerates and low lives in his eyes. Jekyll follows Jinny as she goes through a door into a private office and she pours him a fresh drink.
"Thank you" he takes the drink and has a nervous gulp of it. She wonders over to a safe and takes out an ornate canister. It contains the tigers blood which she places it in front of the now sat down Dr Jekyll in a chair at her desk. "This is what you need Dr Jekyll, but the price goes up each time. It's becoming even more rare than it used to be."

"Miss Wu, I appreciate this, but I won't have the money until next week" Dr Jekyll spent a little too much at the table before she got there and now the price increase. He wasn't in a position to argue though.

"Don't worry Doctor. Come back within fourteen days and pay me, there's no problem." Jinny Wu says as she sits down and takes a sip of her drink. "But don't let me down." she warns in a calm manner.

"Of course Miss Wu" he stutters as he gets up and puts on his coat. He walk to the door of the room clinging on to the canister, he gently caresses it into his pocket like its a precious stone or a bomb that has to be handled with extreme care. "Thank you" He utters as he opens the door.

"Don't let me down Dr Jekyll, you won't like me when I'm cross." He gives a curt nod and leaves the room back into the main casino. He sits and plays two more games of blackjack before cashing in his chips and leaving the casino and heads home. He simply couldn't wait any longer. the Serum has to get into his system before Hyde came back again.

Once he returned home he went straight to his basement to work on the serum. He did not want Mr Hyde making an unexpected appearance. He pulls out the ancient looking book and starts to concoct a formula whilst muttering to himself. Part willing it to work and part making sure he gets the recipe right. Of course he wont know if it works until he has had it in his system for a little while, but he had convinced himself it would work. He takes the serum, and he injects it because it hits the blood stream quicker, although as usual he feels no different immediately.

He drags himself to the chair and sits down, needing to think of a new password. He looks in a murky mirror and sees the words from the night before. Gorge, gullet, larynx, pharynx. Hyde has never noticed the words behind them but Dr Jekyll hopes that even if he did, he wouldn't guess what they mean. He changes it daily so has to make sure he remembers it. He walks over to the board and rubs them out and starts writing cosmos, orb, globe, planet before walking to the basement door and unlocks it - the doctor was due to come again this evening. He then sits back in the chair, takes a couple of sleeping pills knowing that the Serum would take a day or two to take hold if it did work. He secured himself and pressed a button "Earth" he said, and then repeated. "Earth" the lock instantly tightened to the point where he can't manoeuvre his arms. He drifts off into a deep sleep. After three hours Dr Carmichael walks in the unlocked basement as previously agreed with Dr Jekyll. She had been warned that Hyde may not come to play - it depends on the effects of the serum. The Doctor feels attached to the case already, she already feels emotionally invested. She takes a seat closer to Dr Jekyll this time, she assumed it was still Jekyll until Hyde announces himself. She inspected him at close quarters while he's sleeping. His hair ruffled and smelt of whiskey, shirt untucked and trousers not as neat as usual.   She pulls out her smart phone and starts to make notes while she waits for Hyde to awake from Jekyll's subconscious.

Luckily she has patience, the sleeping pills certainly worked their magic but sure enough Hyde stirred and awoke in the shadows of darkness. She didn't notice him awakening. He looked at hear with bleary eyes and saw her making notes. "You must really like him." said Hyde. "They never usually come back" he tells her.
"How many have there been?" She asks as he takes a large over exaggerated breath through his nose "And You've changed your perfume." he notices and completely ignoring her question. She feels uncomfortable that he could make such an

observation and quips back not in her usual character "while you smell like a distillery." He lets out a little chuckle knowing he has got under her skin a little. "Tired are we doctor?" He continues to poke the proverbial bear.
"How many?" She repeats like a possessive girlfriend inspecting a new partners previous conquests.
"Not many," he continues, "not very many at all, he's not very trusting, of course not many people are understanding of our special circumstances."
"I understand that" she says. "I have been thinking Mr Hyde, what you said about being free, expressing yourself, you do know he's trying to eradicate you completely?" she tries to put him in the picture.

"Ah yes, the serum." He laughs in a sinister manner. "Don't worry, I have grown a tolerance to those ingredients. In fact, I think it just makes me more prevalent now. He got rid of me for two years before using a similar concoction, but then needed me to help him out of another problem he got himself into."
"Problem?" Doctor Carmichael probed.
"This time it is was with a drug gang in Manchester. He poked his nose in where is doesn't belong and when it goes wrong, he calls on me. He can't be without

me....he thinks he can, but when he falls over, he needs me to pick him up." He tells the Doctor. She stands up and walks over to him and checks the locks on his wrists. "It's a pretty secure system he has here" she says.

"Certainly is. I once said the password by fluke, I basically said every word I could think of in a 4 hour timeframe and it pinged open." He looks up at her longingly like she would be able to magic the shackles away. No such magic.

Now he changes it every day, god knows how he remembers what the code is every morning." he regales the doctor with his story. She looks at him with empathy. "You could always help me with the password" he says hopefully still looking up with those puppy dog eyes. She walks away from him and gets a bottle of water from the work desk and opens it "You know I can't do that Mr Hyde." she offers him some of the water which he opens his mouth and allows her to pour some water in, some spills down his chin, so she leans over to grab a tissue and clean it up. She is very close at this point, almost like she wants him to break free and pull her in tight. He swallows the water and takes a deep breath inhaling her perfume particles "Then, please, Doctor, why on earth are you here?" He says slowly as looks away as if to detach from her conversation.

She hears the clunk of the restraints first and is frozen to the spot as the restraints fall by the side of the chair and he stands up to match her. He is a good 3/4 of a foot taller then her. Now looking down on her with a wry smile on his face.
"Well, would you look at that?" He says. The doctor takes a deep gulp and speaks in a shaky voice
"I think you should sit back down Mr Hyde. I want to help you."
"Please, I could have snapped your neck the moment the shackles fell." He explains hovering his giant hand over her slender neck, he can almost hear the fear coursing through her veins. He stretches letting out a mighty roar, it's been a while since he was able to do that. He weighs up his options, but not for a great deal of time. When you haven't been allowed out for a long time, you're going to go out. When Jekyll goes out and has fun Hyde feels none of it. Not even the memory of it. "I'm going for a walk. If you're still here when I return, we can talk."

"Mr Hyde, if you leave you break any trust thats building."
"I'll be back Carmichael, If you're still here when I get back we can have a good chat then... you know, about my feelings and that." he says mockingly as he skips to the door that leads out to the street. Carmichael still frozen to the spot she was in, still completely dumfounded by the events that have just taken place. She takes out her phone as if to ring someone and tell them, but who is she going to tell? She eventually peels herself from the spot she was stuck to and runs to the door. He is out of sight completely.
"Shit." She sits back in her chair and waits for the inevitable. Dr Jekyll won't be happy she thought.

CHAPTER FOUR

A FREE MAN

So what does one do once set free? For the first time in years? Mr Hyde almost had no idea what to do. If you listened to Dr Jekyll's stories, he would have already murdered three innocent people and robbed a bank. But we know this not to be the case. He walked the streets, watching normal people go about their night. Of course there weren't many of them around at 3am, but a few to watch. Not a great deal for a super strength, over-protective alter ego to do at this point, you can kind of see Dr Jekylls point on this! Chaos seems to follow boredom.

Either way, Hyde is happy not to have the restraints around him. Even now though, he can still feel tightness where they usually are. Hyde was thinking rationally. If he simply went out to enjoy himself and does something stupid, he gets found out and damages the relationship with Jekyll and Carmichael further. Or, he could simply be more reserved, go back to the basement and build trust. He decides to enjoy an hour of freedom walking through the local park which was deserted. Strange people are scared of the park at dark he thought. No one is here. He decides to do what he and Dr Jekyll love doing, consume some whiskey. So he pops to the off license which is open 24 hours. Luckily his fingerprint ID still works on Dr Jekylls phone so paying for things was easy enough.

He enters the off license and walks over to the back of the store where some of the spirits were. The shopkeeper doesn't say a word as she is half asleep and Hyde makes no effort as he would rather people didn't talk to him. His senses are heightened but his conversation isn't what it used to be. As he is choosing what bottle to buy he hears a stirring at the counter. Jekyll always buys the same, Hyde thought a different bottle might give him a bad head in the morning so chooses something new with a slight chuckle to himself about the thought of Jekyll being hungover in the morning. Hyde looks around to the counter as the noise was intensifying to see a man pointing a gun at the helpless young shop assistant. The man wearing an ill-fitting balaclava and a white hoody was waving the pistol around shouting at her to hurry up. From the height, build and tattoos on his hands, it looks like Deano. Perhaps trying to scavenge the money together that he owes Tony. Hyde look at the floor and shakes his head

"Just what I fucking need." He knew he simply wouldn't be able to stop himself. He walks over to the gunman, who quickly turns the gun on Hyde before he gets too close to him, making Hyde stop dead in his tracks. Hyde smiles at him thinking it may help the situation.

"You should leave." Hyde advises the stocky man.
"Just go along your way pal. No one needs to get hurt." The gunman advises Hyde, who could sense a quiver of fear in his voice.

"I can't do that, this is my local shop you see. Why don't you just leave calmly?" *while you still can* he thought.

"I'll give the orders here! I'm the one with the gun shit for brains." he shouts as he lifts up his I'll fitting balaclava to reveal Deano's face, wide eyed and clearly panicked. Hyde was going to let him go, but this sought of behaviour really made him mad.

"So you do." Hyde says as he weighs up the options and places the bottle of whiskey gently on the floor. Quicker than the man can react Hyde grabs the gun and lurches at the attacker, head butting him to the floor. Blood spills from his nose has he falls. Hyde with his wits about him then proceeds to make sure the gun is far enough away that its safe and then grabs the man by his ears and smashes his head on the floor repeatedly until blood starts pouring from the back of his head.

The lady behind the counter screams and Hyde snaps out of his own violent trance. He stands up and looks at the woman. "Please can you stop shouting?" he asks of her slowly and deliberately. She does so and holds it in. Hyde takes a deep breath and smashes Deano's head a few more times for good measure hearing the squelching and skull smashing on the tiled floor. He stands up and straightens himself out, grabs his bottle and walks back to the counter. The lady is in such a state he doesn't bother trying to pay "I was never here...You understand me?" He says staring through her thick glasses and streaming tears. She trembles and tries to nod as he walks out, leaving Deano on the floor with blood still pouring from the back of his head. "Unbelievable." he mutters to himself as he opens the bottle and takes a drink, walking in the general direction of his house.

He has the conversation in his mind over and over again. How does he convince Carmichael that his isn't what it seems. Jekyll has told her what would happen and now its happened. Foregone conclusion. He sat on a bench underneath a light in the park. He could see the house from the bench, with a small singular light emanating from the basement. If she was even still there? The conversation would be much easier if the weren't.

He walks in to see the doctor, blood splattered over himself and with an opened, half drunk bottle of whiskey. Of course, she wont buy his story. "What did you do Mr Hyde?" She asks in an accusatory tone. "You wouldn't believe me if I told you" he tells the Doctor. "Try me" she says sitting in his usual chair inviting him to sit in her chair, showing the trust she has in their relationship. Hyde liked this doctor, maybe she would understand. Maybe she could help.

"I helped a shopkeeper who was being held up at gun point." He told her very nonchalantly as he slumped in her usual chair.
"Mr Hyde, I really want to help you but you have to be honest with me."
"I told you that you wouldn't believe me." he tells the doctor. He usually likes to be right, but there are some exceptions.
"You can see how it looks can't you Mr Hyde?" she says as she get up and walks around the basement.
"Of course, I have a very high IQ doctor, I know it looks like I have escaped, got drunk and murdered someone simply exasperating the opinion already imparted on you from our good friend Dr Jekyll." Hyde explains showing he is not inept of the interpretation of his actions.

He slumps back in his chair and puts the loose restraints around him. "Go ahead, push that button and say any word twice. It will only respond to your voice after that so you are safe." Hyde continues knowing he has breached any trust they may have built. She sits down in her chair and stares at the sorry state of Hyde. This is not how a psychopath behaves, she thought to herself. But she is still wary. "Is that the truth of the matter Mr Hyde?" she asks.

"Yes. I know you won't believe it. I know the reputation that has been created for me." He says in a sad voice.

"There will be a mess to clear up tomorrow" she explains with a sympathetic voice. "I would suggest you get back in your restraints ready for the morning. Why not leave Dr Jekyll a note to explain. I will leave you to it." She gets up and leaves him.

"You are leaving me unshackled?" He asks confused
"You said you wanted to do the right thing Mr Hyde. Here's your chance." She says as she smiles at him and puts her coat over her shoulders. Think about it. She slams the door behind her and he was once again alone. Mr Hyde decided to take her advice and write a note. He wrote two or three as his sticky blood stained hands kept ruining the paper he was writing on. In the end he just wrote "I didn't mean to." He knew Dr Jekyll would not understand he was trying to do the right thing but at least he was trying. He went and quickly washed his hands with some hand wash but there was still some blood on his clothes that he couldn't get off. If he went and got changed, Jekyll would know. He sat

down and secured the shackles once again and locked it "Earth" he said twice over while holding the button to lock him to the chair. He wouldn't struggle and fight tonight. Jekyll would have enough to sort out tomorrow. He closed his eyes and drifted off to sleep with the thoughts of the doctor and her belief in him soothing him to sleep.

The next morning Dr Jekyll woke feeling less tired than usual. His limbs were not aching from the usual struggle. Immediately he assumes the serum has taken affect and Mr Hyde was kept at bay. He didn't even see the note, he went over to the lab to portion up his serum into daily doses. He felt light on his feet, almost dancing around the lab. He doesn't even notice the dirty bloodstained clothes he's in as he strips off for a shower. Today is the first day in years he hasn't needed two or three coffees before he can muster the energy to get in the shower. Today he has been asked to make an appearance at a charity ball for under privileged children. As a (mainly) well respected doctor he still has to make these appearances rather than just recluse into a life of emptiness and internal battles.

He gets himself dressed in a lovely navy suit and a light pink shirt. He deliberated over a blue or a black tie before springing out of the door and walked towards the convention centre where the event was being held. He comes to a crime scene thats closing off the road that he would usually use. A shop seems to have had an altercation. Dr Jekyll clasping his black and silver briefcase in his left hand was desperate to know what had happened but was in a rush. He hated being late. "Is everything ok here?" He asked the tall policeman who was minding the crime scene from the other side of the crime tape as it rattled and flapped in the wind. "Nothing for you to concern yourself with sir" he batted back in a very serious tone. His fluorescent jacket occasionally reflecting the sun back into Jekyll's eyes. Dr Jekyll looked at the shop "I'm sorry" he mutters out loud without realising. "Pardon me sir?" the police officer looked down at him. "Er, nothing. Sorry for the situation, looks nasty" he turns on his heels and marches back to his house. What was that? Was it Hyde? Was it him speaking on behalf of Hyde? He felt sick to the core.

He entered the basement to take another shot of the serum. He went through his draws rapidly and in a panic. As he is frantically searching he notices bloodstained note on the side. "I didn't mean to" it read.

"HYDE!!" He shouts! "What did you do? How did you escape?" His shaking hands rattle through the cupboard as he frantically tries to load more serum into his system. He picks up a small mirror and stares into it. WHAT DID YOU DO?" frantically and in a fit of panic by now.

"I didn't mean to" he hears himself say. "I was trying to help"

"I'm talking to myself, this is insane" he says over and over to himself. He injects himself with the serum again in the hope that it keeps him at bay. As the needle goes in he shudders and presses the plunger to deliver the extra shot of serum. He locks all of his doors and puts himself in the restraints in a panic. "Pumpernickel" he says twice over holding down the button, he went back to random words because he had no idea how Hyde guessed the last one. Maybe he saw the words on the board. He waits. He waits longer. Every imaginable thought went through his head as he sat there. An hour passed, then another. Not a word. "SHOW YOURSELF HYDE!" he exclaims but nothing. He soon drops off to sleep in the slumber of the chair. It was high backed with a comfy headrest, he had it amended so he didn't have such a bad neck in the morning. The chains never got any more comfortable though.

A knock at the house door wakes him from his dream state. Suddenly all the fog clears from his head, thinking clearly, no sign of Hyde. He unlocks the restraints and makes his way upstairs, making good of the house as he goes, straightening things out as a second knock at the door comes. He opens the door to a uniformed officer - a different one to the one he saw earlier. "Hello sir, there has been an incident at the store round the corner sir and we are conducting house to house calls to see if anyone saw or heard anything last night?" he said. He was much shorter than the last officer and no where near as formal.

"Oh that's terrible. Not a peep I'm sorry" he said very calmly. "Can I ask what happened?" Dr Jekyll enquired.

"Someone interrupted a robbery and killed the assailant." He said in a very casual but matter of fact way.

"Wow, um, no, I am sorry. Did anyone get a good look at who did it?"

"Tall with dark hair, doesn't narrow it down much does it, the shopkeeper was in shock. It could be you for all we know!" He pauses before laughing and Dr Jekyll joins in despite the sick feeling churning around in his stomach. "Personally, he sounds like a hero to me, taking down scum like that, but rules is rules! We have to investigate." he states. Jekyll's mind wonders to thoughts of Hyde being hailed as a hero "So you saw nothing sir?" the officer rudely interrupted his thoughts.

"No, sorry, I slept really well and didn't even stir I don't think." Dr Jekyll told the officer.

"Thank you anyway sir" he says as he walks away whistling and into the next door he goes. Dr Jekyll closes the door and crumples at the foot of it. "What have I done?" he mutters to himself. "Hyde." he says again with clarity. "What has Hyde done?" he scurries back to his feet and goes back to the basement.

When he gets down to the basement he sees the doctor approaching the door through the small window. He storms over and lets her in. "We're you here last night?" He asks with urgency.
"I was." The doctor answers him, she knew this would come up, the reason for her visit. She knows a barrage is coming her way.
"What happened?" Jekyll asks with open arms as if to invite a response.
"He didn't mean to harm anyone!"
"Now you're taking his side?"
"No, but I saw how he was afterwards. He was trying to help." She is not sure why she's taking Hyde's side on this but she is.
"If he truly wanted to help" Jekyll pauses and really thinks about what he is going to say "then he would disappear forever!" Jekyll stormed past her and walked up the steps and away from the house like a sulky teenager going to his room.
"Where are you going?" She shouts after him
He doesn't answer through fear of saying something he can't take back. He is determined to blow off some steam. He makes his way back to the casino.

He gets to the steel door and suddenly remembers he owes Miss Wu some cash. "Shit." he mutters to himself. He takes a deep breath and opens the steel door. He gets let in through the other steel door and sits down at an empty table. Just him and the croupier at the start, this time it's roulette. He places down some money as a drink is brought over to him. No sign of Miss Wu he thinks to himself, probably a good thing. He drinks his drink quickly and signals to the waitress for another, she sees him and seemed to understand his request. He seems to have settled in for the night and not wanting Mr Hyde to make an appearance. Even better, he seemed to be winning some money. Maybe his debt could be settled after all. Maybe something good could have come from this atrocity. His mind wondered back to Hyde.

Why interrupt the robbery? Why did the doctor let him go? Did she help him? HIs mind was swirling with questions when Miss Wu came and sat next to him.
"Dr Jekyll" she said catching him off guard "I wasn't expecting you a few more days"
"Ah yes, well I have most of your cash, so wanted to drop it in to you" he fumbled to an answer on his feet. He took some cash and a few of his chips and slid them over to her.
"Thank you Dr. You can drop the rest in later in the week" she tells him and wonders off amongst the

other punters that are in her casino. It's maybe half as busy as it was last time he came in. After another hour of hits and misses at the table he decided to knock it on the head and walk home. He left the casino and took a walk by the ship yard. It was a nice scenic detour home.

He meanders half drunk, half perplexed past the docked ships and containers when he hears an altercation. There are raised voices he can hear, so Jekyll hides himself against a container where he cant be seen. He leans around the corner to see who it is. There is a man in a smart suit doing most of the shouting in a thick welsh accent which he can just about make out.
"I am not paying for this. It's not what we agreed. I wanted European , not black!" he shouts. Jekyll has seen the man in the casino before. Tony he thinks his name is. "This is what we agreed last week Tony" Miss Wu states in a shrill voice. She is frightening at the best of times.

The argument continues and Dr Jekyll knows he needs to leave. He spins back from where he came from and jogged away. Once he was far enough away he pulled out his phone and made a phone call to the local police station. He advised them to have a snoop around the casino. He felt like it was the right thing to do, unsure of exactly what he saw, but he knew it wasn't a good thing. When he returned home the basement door was not locked but the doctor had left. He reflected on their argument. He knows he shouldn't have reacted like he did but he got so worked up. Dr Jekyll locks the house and secures himself in the usual way. "Tomorrow will be a better day." he assures himself.

CHAPTER FIVE

A DOCTOR OF PSYCHOLOGY

Doctor Carmichael very rarely took on work that wasn't for a private client. No hospital work, she did her time in that business, now she likes to be well paid for the work she does. Now she tends to work along side clients like Dr Jekyll, specialist cases. They pay well so she keeps going with them for as long as they interest her. She lives in a nice penthouse in London city centre with views over the city. It's very minimalistic like you would expect from a clinical person, everything has its place. Everything is clean and tidy. The dark stained oak bookshelves are by far the the oldest thing in the apartment which is full of books. As you would expect, they are organised by category. Work books take the top two shelves - all of the books she has used to learn how to be the very best at what she does. The next shelf is self development with some audio books, she is clearly very into continuing her personal growth. The rest of the shelves are made up of fiction books, she loved to read fiction. Dealing with facts and peoples lives daily, she needed an escape, her books did that for her. Reading the terrible trials and tribulations of people who were not real, gave her a certain amount of satisfaction. Escapism also came in by way of reality TV, her self professed guilty pleasure.

She met Dr Hyde at a conference they were both invited to attend. She was the key note speaker at the event with around 2,000 attendees. She was well respected by her peers and people looked up to her and her opinions. Dr Jekyll was one of those people who looked up to her. After the event he asked if she would like a drink as he would like to speak to her about a sensitive matter. "Nothing like that." Doctor Jekyll wanted to reassure her. He hadn't had a girlfriend for a very long time as you can imagine. Hyde didn't make it easy to have a meaningful relationship, although the odd none- meangful one didn't go amiss   Women came and went, but no one he could call a girlfriend, he had pretty much resigned himself to a life on his own. She accepted his invite and they went for dinner and a drink and the restaurant within the hotel.

"I would like to talk to you about a sensitive subject, psychologically speaking" Jekyll managed to get past the starter with small talk before he wanted to get down to the real reason for their sit down. But how do you tell someone something like this. It's not like he has dark thoughts every now and then. He would rather be in an even more secluded setting but he know that would be unlikely - and he wouldn't feel comfortable asking. The restaurant was pretty big, maybe 70 tables in all. They were sat in a corner with a black table cloth draped over the table with red napkins. It was well lit with a young woman playing the piano. The menus were just a crisp white piece of paper with lots of fancy words and some big numbers next to the £ sign. But neither Jekyll or Doctor Carmichael were short of any money.

"What is it?" She asked as she sipped her red wine. Still in her suit from delivering her speech earlier. "I'm not really sure how to say it." Jekyll admits. This obviously isn't the sort of thing he talks to other people about on a regular basis.

"It's ok, tell me. I wont judge" She promises Dr Jekyll who scoffs in response and raises one eyebrow.
"That's what you say now." he tells her. "You will definitely judge when I tell you the situation, but here goes." he take a deep breath and a huge gulp of his beer.
"I have an ... alter ego" he starts. "Someone else takes over my body and behaves in a very different way to what I do usually." He clumsily gets the words out.
"We all have a bit of that inside of us Dr Jekyll, its human nature." She tells him. Some rare free advice from the Doctor. "We all feel like someone else controls us at times."
"No, I mean actually controls me." He tries to take her further down the rabbit hole.
"I'm not sure I follow? Takes over your thoughts?"
"Everything. Body and mind. I can't remember a single thing that's happened." He goes on to tell her. "I have created some medication to subdue him but it doesn't always work."
"Him? You refer to it as another person."
Jekyll suddenly realises how bizarre its sounding when he says it all out loud. "Well, yes. Mr Hyde. Its easier for me to compartmentalise it." he reasons.
"Do you speak to him too?" The doctor chuckles as she asks.

"This was a bad idea, I'm sorry." He starts to get up, clearly embarrassed that he had entrusted her with his biggest secret only to be laughed at.
"No, please, sit" She asks him. "I am intrigued." He sits back down gingerly and takes another big gulp of his beer.

"On the surface, there are many many things this can be attributed to. schizophrenia, multiple personality disorder or plain black out and paranoia."
"This is not any of that. It's deeper than that" He argues.
"Dr Jekyll, if you want to commission me to work with you, then come by my office and we can chat formally." They finish their meal making small talk and trying to avoid the subject. Dr Jekyll calls her a taxi and then takes the walk home himself.

Carmichael gets back to her penthouse and is still intrigued. Not like her, she has so much experience and has been there and seen it all ... but this really peaked her interest. She scans over her books to see if she has heard of anything similar. Most of these books she knows from front cover to back - nothing. She sits down and puts some of her reality TV on while she pours herself a glass of wine. Its only a small glass, what was left in the bottle. She didn't want to open a new bottle this late at night. As she finished her wine she closed her eyes for a second, it was getting late and she would often have a little snooze on the sofa before going to bed. Like a pre sleep nap if you like. She dreamt of Dr Jekyll.

She dreamt of Jekyll in a burning building, smoke everywhere, flames licking every window. Although it was a dream, she was sure she could smell the smoke. Jekyll was just standing amongst the flames while the chaos went on around him. He was just staring at himself in a mirror. The mirror image was screaming at him to get out and save himself, but he just stood there staring as if nothing was going on around him. The ceiling collapsed on Jekyll and she shot up suddenly awake. She was sweating, boiling hot as if she was in the room herself while it was on fire. She looked around her calm and peaceful penthouse and gathered herself together. She picked up her phone and text Jekyll "Dr Jekyll, thank you for your time today, can we meet for breakfast tomorrow? Same hotel?." She needed a shower before she went to sleep, her clothes were still smoke stenched, she was sure if it.

She went to breakfast with a certain amount of trepidation. She knew she was meant to help Dr Jekyll, but the dream really shook her up. Does she know how to help him? Dr Jekyll was already waiting patiently at the table with a pot of tea. They were a few tables away from where they were at the evening before. "Thank you for coming." the doctor says as she approached Jekyll.
"No, thank you." he says standing up out of courtesy.
"This is going to sound really strange, but I think I am meant to help you Dr. I had a dream last night which was so vivid."
"What happened?" He asked.
"The details don't matter too much, only that I am clear that we met for a reason. Now, tell me about Mr Hyde."
"Tell you about him?"
"Yes, I mean how does he differ from you?"
"Well" he begins after taking a second to clear his throat. "The most important aspect is that he has what you would call super strength, four or five times

stronger than I am. He heals quicker, his reflexes and senses are heightened." Jekyll tries to explain. The Doctor is just watching the words pouring out of his mouth. She has dealt with some complicated cases but nothing of this magnitude.

The waiter came over and offered some breakfast. They order - Jekyll an omelette and Carmichael a full english.
"So what's next?" Jekyll asks her feeling much more at ease about the situation today.
"Well, I would like to sit down and talk, a good interview session."
"We can do that now..." Jekyll keen to get things started.
"Not with you," she hesitates, "with him." She tells him much to his surprise.

The rest of breakfast was spent with the Doctor convincing Dr Jekyll that spending time with Mr Hyde was the only way to get this process started. She needed to see this for herself, understand it for herself. "Letting you spend time with him alone is not a good idea Doctor, he can be very persuasive and more to the point, deadly." Jekyll warns her in a quiet tone to ensure no one around them hears the conversation.

"You approached me to take this on Dr Jekyll, if you want to do this, we do it my way" Carmichael reaffirmed her stance on the situation. The waiter interrupted their conversation with the delivery of the breakfast, it was exactly as ordered. Dr Jekyll poured two cups of tea whilst the Doctor started on her sausages and eggs - she was ravenous. The dream must have made her particularly hungry.
"Ok, one meeting, we see how it goes."
"Good. Where shall we meet?"
"Mr Hyde spends the evenings in my basement."
"In the basement?"
"Yes, come to the house around 1am the day after tomorrow and you can meet him. But please, don't be shocked by what you see." Jekyll warned as he tucked into his omelette. He slid a business card across the table which had his home address on it. They continued their breakfast in relative silence as Jekyll wondered what the outcome would be.

Once the doctor returned home she was still intrigued so went back over some old books of hers. All the chapters and relevant information she could find about split personality and related topics. She pours herself some wine and drops four texts on to her study desk. She flicks through pages and makes notes upon notes. Occasionally she will go to the computer for some more information, but largely relying on the textbooks that she has on the subject matter. Back to her university days, studying and researching. She suddenly had a hit of nostalgia. The endless nights studying and drinking, red bull and chomping pro plus to keep her going through the night. Loud music to help her study. She loved her university days. She shared a house with two other psychology students who unfortunately didn't stay the course, she ended up living and studying alone. Perhaps this is why she prefers life alone now. She can have everything just as she wants it and no one can judge her or criticise her. She always knew not to let other people's thoughts bother her, but that didn't mean they didn't. Everyone has their own demons to fight.

The next day was much of the same. She must have read every single case to do with split personality or schizophrenia out there. She was determined to fully understand this and help the doctor, it was her new purpose. If she could solve this case there was nothing she couldn't do. Maybe a Nobel prize was on the horizon, she dreamed. She eventually packed up and put all of her books back and turned her computer off. She washed up her wine glass and hit the sack. It was only 5pm but she had a big meeting with her new client (or two) at 1am and she wanted to be at her best.

CHAPTER SIX

DON'T FIGHT IT

The chief of police was an older gentleman. Caring and kind but has a stern way about him when he needs to. Must be in his fifties but still loved to get out into the field. He would always wear the uniform - perfectly pressed, no creases! He felt a little out of place going to the grubby underground casino with a couple of uniformed officers. They knocked on the outer door to which there was no answer of course. They waited for 30-40 seconds before one of the officers opened the door and went through. The next door was locked and they gave it a knock. The little slot opened and a pair of eyes peered out and then closed again before anyone could say anything. It then reopened with two pairs of eyes and closed again very quickly.
"Could you open this door please?" The chief asked still very politely and professionally. He heard a

clunking of metal as the door opened fully revealing the casino behind it. The casino itself was not illegal, but some of the folk in there looked like they were into some illegal stuff. The police officers went for a wonder about the tables while the chief went to the bar. Frankie was working behind bar as she was most nights. Talk, slim, tight dress to show off her best asserts to get the men to drink more and leave generous tips.
"How can I help you sir?" She asked. It was a basic bar with only two drinks on tap and a variety of spirits behind.

"We have had some complaints about unscrupulous behaviour emanating from this premises" the chief said rather bluntly. "We thought we would have a look around, I assume that's ok."
In truth it was a phone call from a half cut anonymous person in the early hours of the morning, but the chief was diligent.
Frankie looks shocked. "Please, sir, we are an upstanding business. We can't account for the behaviour of our customers but we try to do everything we can to be considerate to the local residents." It all sounded very well rehearsed. Exactly

what Jinny Wu would have instructed her cronies to say if the law ever came snooping around.

"Well, we shall just have a quick look around and will be on our way if thats ok?" The chief asked.

"Of course sir. Would you like a drink?" She remained composed.

"Not on the job thank you." The chief remained professional as you would expect. He turned around and saw the officers chatting to the punters, there were only about twenty people in, which is more than the chief thought there would be given the time of day. I guess thats the things with casinos - it could be anytime once you are inside. No windows - no clocks. The chief doesn't allow himself much time for such activities.

He notices the door leading to Jinny's office. "What's in there?" he asks nosily directing his voice back to Frankie

"That's the managers office." Frankie says with a little less composure than before.

"Could you open it?" He asks.

"I don't have a key I am afraid." Frankie responding how Jinny would have wanted her to.

Jinny is watching on CCTV from her office, horrified that they have had the gall to come into her premises unannounced and start snooping around. She watches on as they try and ruffle feathers and quiz the locals. She knows no one will say anything about what goes on here. Most of them don't know and the others are too loyal or too scared to say anything. She spots the chief walking towards the door and reaching for the handle. He places his hand on the handle and tries it. "Locked" he says. Jinny can see the handle turning from her side of the door.
"I did tell you sir." Frankie told him.
"Yes, you did." The chief said, looking at her suspiciously. "Come on guys, lets head out. Thank you for your hospitality" he was always raised to have good manners, even if they were disingenuous.
"You''re welcome sir. Have a nice day." She sees them out of the door and closes it behind them.

The last few mornings have been great for Dr Jekyll. No aches, pains or signs of killing people. What more could a man ask from his alter ego?! He has a meeting with the doctor today. He thinks he is ready to say goodbye to her. The daily serum seems to be working and no sign of Mr Hyde.

After a much more upbeat morning routine than he's used to, he heads to the dining room and prepares some tea. Whistling as he goes. He puts the kettle on to boil and fetches the milk from the fridge. He felt nervous about saying good bye to the doctor, but maybe she would like to see him in a social capacity. He sits down and waits. She's not late, but she's usually early, so he wants to be ready. Dr Jekyll sits in his open neck shirt with no jacket today. A bit more informal than usual, but he is feeling good. He hears a knock at the door and springs over to the door to let Carmichael in.
"Come in Doctor" he says in a chirpy voice.
"You're rather chipper today? She notices.
"Thank you Doctor. I am. Things are progressing really well" He really is feeling on top of the world
"Tea?" he offers. He starts to pour before he gets an answer.
"So tell me, why so happy today Dr Jekyll?"
"He's gone." He announces
"Gone, what do you mean gone?"
"Gone. He hasn't been here for the last couple of nights"
"Just like that?" The doctor seems concerned.

"Well, the serum i have devised appears to be working" he proudly tells her.
"You must be careful Dr Jekyll, the tolerance may soon build back up"
"I can feel it Doctor, he's gone."
"Please. Exercise caution" she warns him as she drinks her tea.
"So, I fear that I no longer need your services Doctor"
"I can't help but feel that's unwise Dr Jekyll. You have gone through much trauma."
"I don't need counselling Doctor. I am good as new" he exclaims.
"Well, I will pop in on you from time to time, as a friend to make sure you are ok?"
"That's kind of you Doctor. Maybe I can make you dinner one night?"
"Maybe" She says as she stands up and leaves the room toward the front door. "Take care of yourself Dr Jekyll" she says just before she leaves.

He sits at the table pleased with himself, for a short while before popping to the local shop to get todays papers and some whiskey. He arrives at the shop which of course is now fully back up and running with the crime tape taken down and the police officers all departed. He walks in and the door makes a typically dull "DING" as he enters. A cheap bell set up for the door to connect with as it opens. He chooses two of this favourite papers and his favourite whiskey and proceeds to the counter where the young girl and Sam the shop keeper are standing.

The shopkeeper moves closer to Sam and he puts his arm around her.
"This is the man?" Sam asks the girl. She nods timidly without breaking eye contact with Dr Jekyll. Sam comes out from behind the counter and grabs Dr Jekyll by the hand and shakes it uncontrollably. "You don't pay for anything here sir. Thank you"
"OK..." Dr Jekyll unsure whats going on.
"That man, you saved us! Thank you" Suddenly Jekyll realises what he's talking about.
"I think you have your wires crossed" he thinks on his feet quickly, not wanting this to get back to the police
"You're my hero" the shopkeeper announces
Sam taps the side of his nose" Oh yes of course sir.
"But you still don't pay here" he says as he ushers him out of the shop. Jekyll leaves bemused. Maybe Hyde was trying to do good? He slowly walked back to his home deep in thought. That night he would sleep

unshackled for the first time in years and hope that Hyde would continue to stay away. He goes through his phone and finds the number for Doctor Carmichael and is a little frustrated that it cuts straight to voicemail. "Hi, listen, I have been thinking about Hyde and what you said about trying to help. Perhaps you can pop over tomorrow for a chat?" She picks the voicemail up sometime later while doing some admin on her balcony. She has a little smile to herself and opens a fresh bottle.

Meanwhile by the docks Jinny Wu is conducting her business. Another deal going down. She has three children with their hands bound together with cable ties, poorly fitted dirty clothes badly covering them up. Walking next to them is a guard watching over them, tall with a gun resting on his hip. They must be around 11 years old and all black females. The man standing opposite is in the door way of his Land Rover while his associates hand over the money. Jinny Wu had been people trafficking for many years and has many loyal clients. She has no idea what becomes of the girls nor does she care. So long as she gets paid and the customers keep coming back she is happy. "Thank you for your business" she offers the courtesy but the man remains quiet in the shadows of his car, assumably to remain as discreet as possible. The associates load the girls into the back of the Land Rover.

The Land Rover speeds off away from the docks and Jinny goes to check on the rest of her merchandise. She goes to the guarded shipment container where she is granted access by the military man who opens the container for her and she walks in. It stinks. Human waste, body odour and left over food all concocted together to give a horrible stench that sticks to your nasal passage long after you have closed the door. There are six girls and four boys left in the container. Difference races and colours - she didn't care - as long as she could sell them. She warned them "behave yourselves and you might live through this process." she states in a cold unwavering voice. She leaves the container and tells the man to lock it up. "We have another collection in a couple of days. The Korean boy." she tells him. She walks off back to her casino undoubtably to conduct more appalling business.

Dr Jekyll awakes in the morning in his own bed. Not having slept in his own bed for so many years, he felt great! The comfort of a pillow and a duvet. Not sleeping in clothes. He got up and got in the shower. Another night when Hyde didn't come around - he thinks. He checked his body for breakages and bruises. He checked his wallet and online banking, his wardrobe, the rest of the house. Everything was as it was when he went to bed. How peaceful Dr Jekyll felt. Today he felt like doing a jigsaw puzzle. He used to do them all the time but Hyde would get bored and smash the place up so he had stopped doing them. He went into a very dusty and packed loft where he had them stored. He dug out three puzzles and brought them all down and placed them downstairs on the dining room table. He makes himself a cup of tea and has a sit down before starting to unpack the first of his puzzles.

There is a knock at the door so Jekyll gets up and answers it. "Ah, hi doctor, come in" he says to her "I was hoping you'd come, would you like some tea?" "Er, yes of course" she is unsure how to take this new Jekyll who spoke at 100 miles per hour.

"Are you ok?" She seeks to confirm.
"Never better doctor" he claims.
"What was it you wanted to speak to me about?" She get straight to the point.
"I think Hyde was trying to do good, or at least didn't always mean to cause harm. But, I think we're all good doctor. I don't think we need your treatment anymore." Jekyll informed her.
"What are you talking about Dr Jekyll?" with more than a sense of de ja vu.
"I have cured us" he says smugly.
"Are you ok Dr Jekyll?" She suddenly feels like he's having a break down.
"Better than ever! Did you not hear me?"
"We have been over this yesterday Dr Jekyll." she tells him very bluntly.

Dr Jekyll's face crumbles. He suddenly feels very hot and sick.
"I didn't see you yesterday!" he almost chokes on his words as they escape his body."
"We sat at this very same table and discussed the very same thing!"
There could only be one explanation. "HYDE!" he trembles with anger and fear.

"What?" the doctor still unsure whats going on.
"It was Hyde." he tells her still unable to control his body from shaking.
"You said you'd cured him?" The doctor questions him.
"Obviously not!" He shouts.... "This man" he continues until interrupted
"IS YOU!" The doctor shouts at him. "Hyde is you. You are Hyde. Everything that he does is on some level because of you." she cries. All of her research and her observations spilling out of her.
"This is my fault?" Jekyll suddenly turning on her.
"If you didn't have him held prisoner every night he wouldn't feel the need to go crazy when he can leave would he?" She tells him, not reading the room very well at all. He walks towards her slowly and purposefully. It feels as though the whole room had darkened as he approached her.
"He is a pathological liar, look what he has done to us!"
"Why is it always some else's fault?" She stands up to try and give some distance as he gets closer.
"Dr Jekyll I am asking you to back off" she warns him in no uncertain terms.
 He grabs her by the neck and forces her backwards and onto the floor. She tries to scream but no sound comes out as she open her mouth.
"This is not my fault!" he shouts as he is now choking her with all his bodyweight on her.

Suddenly he feels a force pulling him back and relinquishes his grip for a second but soon regains control. "Stay there Hyde!" He tells his alter ego. He lets go again for longer this time, long enough for the Doctor to push him away and scurry into the corner. Jekyll let's out a mighty scream and jumps up onto the table "Stop interfering!" he shouts. The doctor watches on in silence trying to catch her breath again. She watches perhaps the strangest exchange she has ever witnessed between two men in the same body.
"You don't treat people like that!" Hyde shouted
"You need to stop interfering" Jekyll reiterated his earlier demand.
"You need me to interfere!"
"I don't need anything from you"
Jekyll is shouting these words to himself in a genuine argument with himself. He is moving around the table as he does so. He slips off the side and smashes his head on the side of the table and crumples in a heap on the floor and there is a deafening silence that falls over the house.

The doctor is deadly silent and still cowering in the corner. Having flashbacks to her parents fighting when she was younger and watching from under the dining room table. She seems to end up in these situations more than she should. She waits for a minute or two in the deafening silence that followed such a harrowing ordeal, before struggling to her feet. She knows the access to the basement is in the dining room somewhere, and knowing Dr Jekyll like she does, she assumed it would be a hidden door. She searched the bookshelf, pulling at random books in a panic, her hands still shaking, what if he woke up? Why didn't she just run? She paused and took a deep breath and started again systematically pulling watch of the books in order. Eventually stumbled on a book called "Escapism" which seemed a little heavier than the others. It was the handle to open the door. The secret door popped out of the frame and she peeled it open. She turned on the light and walked down into the familiar space, she could never understand why people in films never bothered turning on lights when they went into basements. She saw the chair where Hyde usually gets tied up in and makes sure the door to the street is locked. Quickly, she turns around and runs back upstairs. She stumbles on the second and third step but her momentum carries her up the rest of the stairs.

She proceeded to drag Dr Jekyll to the door and carefully drags him down the stairs. She struggles as Dr Jekyll was considerably bigger than she was but her sheer willpower sees her through it. She manages to prop him in his chair and took a few seconds to catch her breath. Not taking her eyes off him for a moment as she did. Then she secures the shackles she held down the button and thought of a word that came to her head. For some reason she went back to her first meeting with Mr Hyde. "Perfume, Perfume. " She said. She sat in her chair and reflected on the events that had occurred. Maybe Mr Hyde was telling the truth. Maybe it's Dr Jekyll who gets a thrill out of attacking people and killing people. Maybe it's Dr Jekyll who gets drunk and does outrageous things. Maybe Mr Hyde is the fall guy for the good doctor's bad behaviour.

Dr Jekyll started to struggle and pull at his restraints as he awoke wanting to feel his head where he hit it on the way down. He had a cracking head ache but he

wasn't bleeding thankfully. "It's a clever system you created here Dr Jekyll, there's no way around it."
"You gotta let me out" Dr Jekyll threatened. He had a bruise appearing on his head from where he hit the table. "You probably have concussion, but I think that's the least of the problems in that head of yours." She observed. "Is this history repeating itself Dr Jekyll? Is this what happened throughout the years, you make the mistakes and blame Mr Hyde for your wrong doings, is that where the legend comes from?"
"I'm sorry, I got upset. Just let me out and we can talk about this in a rational manner" Jekyll said now fully back to his senses and fully back to his devious self trying to find a way out to the predicament he finds himself in. He has never been in this contraption without knowing the password before. It's frightening.

"You and Mr Hyde have so much potential. If you could find a way to reconcile and work together you can do some great things."
"Too much water has gone under the bridge for that to happen. I don't think we know how to work together as a team anymore." He says solemnly.

The doctor could see Dr Jekyll starting to sweat, maybe a panic attack starting trapped in his own contraption built to contain a monster.
"I could've just left, but I didn't, I want to help you. I want you to mend your relationship with Mr Hyde"
"He'll never agree to it" Hyde interjected although the doctor could not tell the difference other than Hydes voice has a slight growl to it.
"You'll never agree to it you mean" Jekyll snaps back. "Look at this mess you've got us into now?!" he continues.
"ME? You were the one trying to kill the doctor" Hyde pointed out.
"Fascinating" the doctor says as she watches them argue.
"We are not a science project, let us out" Dr Jekyll demands.
"He won't hurt you, I won't let him." Promises Hyde.
"But please do let us go."

How can she be sure that this isn't Dr Jekyll just being smart? She can't take the risk. She sits back for a few seconds and thinks as they bicker among themselves, a very strange and peculiar thing to observe.

"Stop the arguments" she shouts! "If you can promise to work together I will let you out. No more serums, no more trying to take each other's limelight. You work together." They both be quiet, trying to fathom what she is saying. "Hyde gets time to be free WITHOUT violence. In return Dr Jekyll can lead his life without interruptions" The boys remain quiet. There's a long awkward pause while the boys mull it over.

"I'll leave you to think things over'" she says as she gets up and heads towards the door of the basement. "Wait." She knows it's Jekyll, she is starting to learn the difference between who is talking by the tone and sharpness of the voice. She knows Hyde agrees already. "Ok, I can do that." Jekyll says slowly. The Doctor pauses to weigh up the nature of the offer. "Either of you step out of line, I will expose your secrets to the world. You'll spend the rest of your lives being a science experiment." Their silence speaks volumes. She says the word "Perfume" and the shackles fall away. Jekyll stands up and gets close to her towering over her as he sorts his clothes out. "Don't ever do that again" he says to her and stomps upstairs doing his best teenager impression. The doctor sits in silence alone, proud of what she has accomplished. Maybe they can reconcile and work together.

CHAPTER SEVEN

PEOPLE TRAFFICKING

No matter which way you cut it, no matter which one of them you ask, Jekyll and Hyde will both agree that there are a certain life rules that you stick to. Sure, Dr Jekyll has lived a colourful life, but a lot of that was down to youth or stupidity. Not malice or cruelty. Mr Hyde's atrocities were committed out of necessity rather than desire. Dr Jekyll had a nightmare where the visions of what he saw revisited him. Everyone knows Jinny Wu is involved in some serious dodgy stuff, but selling kids who are most likely slaves or worse, maybe even taken away from their parents against their will. How can someone do that? He can't take on Jinny Wu and her clan single handed and he can't call the police. She's too smart for that. Jinny doesn't know that Dr Jekyll knows about the kids so he chooses to bide his time and decide what to do. Hyde has again been quiet for a few days. The doctor hasn't visited since she tied him up. But they are due to have lunch tomorrow. Dr Jekyll was still concerned that despite the progress that they have made, she may still share his secret. But for today he has another public appearance to make. He has a conference to attend in the city centre. Usually, he wouldn't attend these things out of concern for Hyde's potential appearance. However, Dr Jekyll and Mr Hyde have been on the same wavelength since the incident with the doctor. Dr Jekyll no longer sleeps in shackles. Mr Hyde no longer torments Dr Jekyll. To say they're working In unison would be a stretch, but they are no longer at loggerheads which I guess is what the doctor was bought in to solve, so Dr Jekyll is happy with the outcome.

Dr Jekyll arrives at the convention Centre earlier than needed because he didn't like to be caught off-guard by anything. There are the usual pleasantries to make and the usual people there who comment on Dr Jekyll's recent absence from events, which he simply puts down to illness's. People wouldn't understand if he told them he was having a physical and mental battle with his semi psychopathic and super strong alter ego would they? The event goes off without a hitch. He reconnected with some old friends and even had moments of feeling good… just moments mind. He leaves the convention centre and takes a walk through the park. Hyde's interjections were few and far between and because there is no serum in his system they share some thoughts. Dr Jekyll sits in the park watching kids play with the red and brown leaves that have fallen on the floor in the autumn wind the night before. The weather today is beautiful, no need for a coat or a jumper, just enjoy the sun on your face. There are families feeding ducks to the far right and his thoughts go back to the kids the Jinny Wu is selling.

"You know we have to do something right?" Hyde tells Dr Jekyll. There are no people within earshot to hear him talking to himself luckily.

"What do you suppose we do?"

"We find a way to bring them down"

""Bring them down? Are we James Bond now?"

"No, but we can find a way."

Dr Jekyll gets up and continues the walk home in the autumnal sunshine. He returns home and enters his town house, walks into the sitting room and sits on the sofa. He wasn't one for TV but will happily sit there and read the paper. In fact, he wasn't entirely sure that the TV still worked properly, its been that long. He read the paper still with Hyde's words ringing in his ears.

He gets changed into something more casual. A pair of chinos and a jumper and makes his way to the local pub. He hadn't been here for so long. It hasn't changed, no refurbishment programme here. He sits at the bar, Hyde as usual with him, looking out for him, just like the old days. He orders a beer and sits for a while. The bartender making small talk with the locals. Jekyll looked around the pub. It was a dingy little place with wooden black beams on the ceiling and an open fireplace. Real ale labels attached to the pumps in front of him and some pictures on the wall of various local landscapes. You could just about see the layer of dust on top of the pictures from five metres away. Cleanliness clearly not top of their agenda at this establishment. As he looks around he can't help but recognise some of the low lives from the casino that he has seen there before. He wondered if people looked at him and thought the same thing. He finished his drink and continued to walk home.

Meanwhile at the docks Jinny Wu had another shipment arriving. Maybe drugs, maybe people, only Jinny and her people knew. She approached the container that's just been docked and asked one of the crew to open it. The sun was just going down and the red container seemed to shimmer in the red autumn sun as it set. The man opened the handles one by one with a clanking noise as the metal rubs against the metal and the door opens. There are lots of wooden crates, they must be three foot high and stacked one of top of another. Maybe 40 crates in total. She steps in and one of the men with her opens one of the crates "Not that one" she says in a cold voice "Open that one" she points. The man does as she says. He uses a crow bar to wrench the top of the box away from the body of it. The nails make a screeching noise as they grind against the wood on the way out. The lid is flipped off the box and she reaches in amongst the straw and grabs a gun. A sub machine gun. Black and shiny with no magazine in the bottom of it. "Good" she says. "Put it in number four" she tells him and then heads back to the casino and starts to chat with the punters. She has a big smile on her face, no doubt knowing that she's going to make a fortune on resold military grade weapons on the black market. Her slender figure walks between the tables observing her team at work before she goes and sits besides Tony. "Your delivery is due tomorrow." she tells him.

"Make sure it's the right one this time Jinny" He shows disrespect using her first name, no one called her Jinny but Tony thinks she has been undermining him for months. "It will be as expected." she informs him calmly. "Enjoy your evening." she instructs him as she gets up and walks away to her office. She closes the door and pours herself a drink. One of her guards enters after her. "Let me take care of that fat bastard." the guard asks of her.

"He will get whats coming to him Frank, don't worry." she explains. "Just make sure we are ready for tomorrow."

Tomorrow soon comes and the light peeks through the blinds and shines on Dr Jekylls eyes. Another great nights sleep in his own bed with no shackles. Jekyll (and Hyde) were getting used to this. Jekyll prepares some breakfast. Porridge today. Sometimes he'll get two bowls out by accident. They are living in such unison that its like living with a family member. They talk about the day ahead. "Tonight, we go to the casino and see what we can stir up." Hyde tells Dr Jekyll.

"We are careful though, she is dangerous" Jekyll warns.
"So am I." Hyde reminds his keeper.
Jekyll cleans the house up after breakfast and gets showered and ready. The routine was largely still in place.

As Dr Jekyll approaches the casino he can't help but feel a bit nervous. Concerned maybe, not for him, but for what Hyde might do if provoked. "Stay calm" he tells Hyde as they approach the door and pull it open. As usual, he is let into the casino and handed a drink. It just occurred to Dr Jekyll that this is probably the first time Mr Hyde has been here - that Jekyll knows of. He settles down for roulette, it served him well last time he was there. His whiskey arrived, plenty of ice, just how he likes it. He places £20 worth of chips on a few sporadic numbers, no real strategy. Nothing comes in, so he goes again. Dr Jekyll was not a rich man, but he was smart enough to invest money in certain stocks and shares. It means he always has money, but its not always available to him which is why it took time to pay Jinny Wu last time. Still, all debts settled he was hoping to attract no attention this time. A big guy in a white suit, like something you'd wear to a wedding on the beach sits next to him. Jekyll smells cigar smoke on the man and takes a look. It's Tony. Jekyll didn't know his name but recognised his frame from the docks a few days prior. He was involved in this abhorrent people smuggling ring. Jekyll could feel Hyde getting worked up so he pops to the bathroom. "Calm down, we stand no chance of stopping this if you explode and tear everyone limb from limb do we?" Hyde's silence was a sign of his agreement. He calmly goes back to his table and plays a few more rounds of roulette.

Jinny Wu soon comes out of the door and places her hand on Tony's shoulder while completely ignoring Hyde as if she can see straight through him. Tony drinks his drink and follows Jinny Wu out of the room. Dr Jekyll involuntarily starts to move as Hyde makes his feelings known, he thinks they should follow. But Dr Jekyll knows they need to be more cautious and overpowers Hyde to stay for one more round of roulette before going out the front of the casino. Jekyll slowly and carefully goes round to the side where you can see the ships docked in the bay. All of the shipping containers with whatever ungodly contents are inside them. He listens in as Tony moans about his demands and unhappiness at the way the transaction has been handled so far. Jinny offers a loose apology before getting straight back down to business. "We have what you requested. If you transfer the money the deal can be done"

"I want to see the merchandise first" says Tony. Merchandise thought Dr Jekyll, disgusting. These are small children and he's talking about them like a commodity. Jinny proceeded to bang door of the container where a small boy stepped out, he was Korean just as Tony had asked. "Now we're talking" he said in a disgusting and vile manner, one of his cronies goes and fetches the boy and loads him into the back of Tony's car. Hyde can't watch anymore, he knows his promise to Dr Jekyll, but people like this need to pay. He sprints towards Tony, no one really spots him until last minute.

As one of Tony's cronies tries to pull a gun on him, Hyde punches his arm and breaks his wrist, Hyde then uses the gun to smash his face in and knock him out. Hyde takes Tony by the hair smashes his head into the side of the car, the first time made a hard thudding sound, the second time you could hear it splattered with Tony's blood. The third, Tony sinks to the floor as he can't hold his own body weight anymore. Hyde checks on the kid in the car and carefully closes the car door as if not to disturb a sleeping baby. Someone grabs Hyde and kicks him in the back of the leg to floor him, he retaliates with an uppercut as he raises back to his feet and knocks the man out cold. Two others jump on him before a third tazes him. Hyde finally lays motionless but he can see Jinny Wu walking towards him now he is incapacitated. "Tie him up in there" She instructs her troops as she looks down smiling at the still Dr Jekyll. She takes a rifle from one of the men next to her and smashes it into Jekylls temple to make sure he's unconscious. She laughs as she walks away.

CHAPTER EIGHT

DON'T MAKE HIM MAD

It didn't feel too strange to be tied to a chair after recent events but the surroundings were different for sure. A shipping container. How original Dr Jekyll thought to himself as he feels another open hand smack him across the side of the head. Dr Jekyll was helpless, rope ties his hands and feet to a wooden chair in a shipment container. The container was lit with a strip light along the top in the middle, the door slightly ajar. Two thugs were enjoying slapping him around a bit.
"Don't hurt him too much" Jinny said, "I need him" she says as one of her thugs lays a haymaker into Jekyll's stomach.
"Do you realise what you have cost me?" Jinny asks a bloody Jekyll. "Tony is a huge client for me, and now he's dead. You will pay for this"
Jekyll and Hyde remain silent apart from a moan when they take another punch.

"I want you to secure me £50,000 as compensation Dr Jekyll"

"I don't have that kind of money Miss Wu" Dr Jekyll responded very quickly and calmly.

"Then I suggest you find it. What are you even doing here? This is my business." She tells him.

"We can't allow this to happen" Jekyll explains.

"The kids mean nothing. They are money. They are better here being sold then staying where they are born" Jinny Wu somehow trying to justify her actions.

"Please..." Jekyll asks "Don't make him mad. You can still walk away from this"

"What are you babbling about?" Jinny asks.

"I tried to warn you" Jekyll says as he slumps his head down once again. Just then the whole chair collapses beneath him as if the weight quadrupled and with it the ropes no longer held him in place. He goes for the closest thug and smashed his face into the metal wall, the sound rang throughout the container. He uses the rope thats at his feet to wrap around the second man's neck and repeatedly punch him in the face until he is no longer moving. He turns his attention to Jinny Wu who has already scarpered. The door was wide open and she was no where to be seen. Hyde made off after her in his blood splattered clothes. He leaves the container at pace and starts searching foe her with no sign of her. He sees police sirens coming, someone had obviously heard the commotion and called the police., or maybe this is her trying to set Dr Jekyll up. The car with the kid in it is still there. "Shit, here we go" Jekyll says, "Leave the talking to me yeah" he tells Hyde.

The police cars arrive and Dr Jekyll sinks to his knees and puts his hands on his head. He's not sure why, but he thought this is what you should do. Maybe too many movies when he was younger. Two armed police officers jumped out of the cars, their reflective clothing lit up by the blue flashing lights. Another officer walks over to Dr Hyde and helps him up. "I was here to help, please help the kid in the car" he tells the officer. One of his officers go to the car and see's there is a child in the back, he shouts for support and they wrap a tin foil blanket around him and put him into the back of a police car, Jekyll hoped the car was warm. The police officer took Dr Jekyll to a different car and asked him to get in. "There are more here somewhere" Jekyll told him.

"More what?"

"Children" Jekyll clarifies, still a little in shock at whats gone on.

The car door slams and everything he can hear is muffled but he hears the officer instruct a search of the dock yard. He has done his bit. The officer gets in and drives the car toward the station. Jekyll start's out of the window into the dark, catching glimpses of Hyde in his reflection. "Be calm" he said. "Pardon" the officer asks.
"Nothing." Jekyll says after a pause.

They get to the station and get out of the car. Jekyll slowly walks into the reception of the police station. He has only been here once before, in a very different situation. Hyde got him thrown in the cells for a bar fight years ago. He felt a guilty feeling in the pit of his stomach as he went in, but for once he wasn't in trouble. He was there to help. Having sat in an interview room for twenty or so minutes the police officers wanted to make sure they were 100% clear on what happened.
"So, after tracking down the human trafficking ring, you decided to take it upon yourself to take down four people and rescue the kids all on your own?" The skinnier of the men said.

He was short and skinny man, with a shaved head. Looks like he needs a good meal Jekyll thought. He was wearing a shirt that was too big for him and a blue tie in a Windsor knot. The chubbier of the guys wasn't wearing a tie or a jacket, he was standing over by the window relaxing with a cup of coffee while his partner leads the investigation. Jekyll was not in any restraints, he wasn't under arrest but he had to account for some serious questions that were being asked.

"Yes, the person you are looking for is called Jinny Wu" he told the two men. "She runs the local casino, that's how I got to know the operation in the first place."

"We know Miss Wu." said the larger officer as he walked toward the table and sat at one of the metal chairs. "She is a very generous benefactor for this city and many of its charitable causes"

"Then I would suggest its dirty money" Jekyll quickly responded.

"Are you really trying to tell me" The skinny chap began before being cut off by Hyde "I can only tell you what happened. Choose to believe me or not" he said matter of factly.

"OK, Mr Jekyll, you are free to go for now, please sign this statement and er, just let us know if you're planning on leaving the country would you." the

skinny guy said to him in a slightly more upbeat tone as if to lighten the mood as it clouded over.
"It's Doctor Hyde and don't worry, I am not going anywhere." he reassures the officers as he stands up and tucks the chair back under the table before being let out of the room.

He gets home and is in desperate need of a shower. He goes upstairs and Hyde decides a bath is in order. Dr Jekyll obliges and runs a bath where he can relax and wash away the troubles of the night. What a night. While in the bath he examines a few bruises and cuts he collected. The bath was a lovely, deep, freestanding bath with chrome fittings, the bubbles almost flowing over the edge. He drifted into a perfectly adequate sleep. When he awoke the bath water was tepid and the sun was almost coming up. It had been a busy night and his body ached as he got out of the bath and went to get his head down for a few hours. He was used to not sleeping a great deal, maybe he will have to dust off the coffee machine when he gets out of bed. He draws the blinds and gets into bed after putting on some comfy pyjama bottoms. Some sunshine is still peaking in through the gap in the blinds, but that tends to bother Hyde more than Dr Jekyll. He falls into a deeper sleep than intended but wakes up feeling refreshed. He sits up and his thoughts turn to the kids in that shipment container.

Jekyll gets dressed and heads to the ship yard. He walks past the casino door and continues to the crime scene. There is tape surrounding the area but only one officer in a fluorescent jacket on the other side of the dock not doing a great job of securing the area. Perhaps its the same officer who did the door to door interviews Hyde thought and Jekyll chuckled. He went under the tape and walked over to an empty container with the door open and walked in. No sign of anyone in here. Just a couple of buckets in the corner which made the container stink, Jekyll could only assume what was in them but didn't have the stomach to find out. He left and searched in another two containers, both of which were empty. As he came out of the third one the police officer starting meandering toward him, Jekyll is unsure if he's been spotted but takes off at pace non the less. He slows down round the corner "Where could they be?" Jekyll said a little louder than perhaps intended. "Where do people go when they suffer injury or trauma Hyde asked, working together at last. Hospital thought Jekyll, so he started the walk. It was just over a mile into the city but Jekyll didn't mind the walk. He got to see some interesting people and things along the way.

He approached the hospital and found the entrance among the ambulances and emergency vehicles outside. He didn't want to ask anyone incase it arose suspicion, there were quite a few of them he thought so would hopefully be obvious where they were. He wondered through the cafes and the wards keeping an eye out for the boy he saw when he sees police officers outside one of the wards in the waiting room. He approaches the area thinking this is probably where the boy was being kept. He wanted to check in on him. He felt a little uneasy as he went amongst the police officers who weren't on high alert, just going through paperwork and having a coffee. He was trying to peer into rooms to see if he could see the boy who he had saved. "Hopefully he's ok." Jekyll thought to himself as he scoured the rooms one by one still trying to look inconspicuous. Eventually, he comes across a room with three beds in it, two of them are empty. He is in a room with liaison officers who are making notes and talking about the case. He goes over and talks to the boy.

"How are you?" He asks the boy who has monitoring equipment strapped to him. He doesn't answer but manages to open his eyes briefly to see the man standing over him. He manages a smile.

"Can I help you sir?" one of the liaison officers asks him in a soft voice. She is a tall skinny girl wearing a pencil skirt and a white blouse.

"Sorry, no. I just wanted to see if he's ok?" Jekyll responded.

"You're the man who saved him? He told us about you." She observed.

"No, I didn't er, don't worry." I will catch up with him later.

"He drew this for you. He doesn't speak great English" she hands over a drawing on a scraggly piece of paper. Drawn on it in crayon is a small boy with a giant of a man holding his hand. A small lump finds it way into Jekyll's throat as he can't quite muster the words to say thank you and walks away and out of the hospital.

He takes the route through the park to get home. It's another glorious day and the birds are singing. He walks past the lake watching kids feeding the ducks with their parents. For once he finds himself longing for more. Has he missed out on the years of having a family through his selfish ways? Is this the turning point for him? Where would he start? A 35 year old man who hasn't had a real emotional connection with a woman for over a decade. Except for maybe the doctor. Maybe that's a starting point he thought to himself. He arrives home and his big house never felt emptier. He took the drawing from the kid and put it on his fridge attached by a magnet so he could keep it as a memento. He was not really one for sentiment, but this was different. Jekyll went to his sitting room and opened his paper at the cross word and settled down to relax. It hadn't rained much this summer, but Jekyll noticed there was not a cloud in the sky out of the window. That's the beautiful thing about silence he thought. He decided to send a text to the doctor. "I hope to see you again soon x" it read. He pondered briefly before deleting the message and returning to his crossword.

There is a knock at the door just as Jekyll was nodding off. He drowsily gets up and answers it. It was the

Doctor. "Wow, I mean hi" he stumbles over his words as she stands there in a beautiful summer dress.
"Hi, I just wanted to say thank you for the text and..." she struggles for her words "Well, you said I hope to see you again soon, soooo"
"Yes, yes, er - come in." She comes in and helps herself to a glass of wine from the side. "I wanted to make sure we were ok after the incident last week." he said referring to when he attacked her.
"What's a little life threatening choke between friends ay?" she jokes.
"Don't, I honestly don't know what came over me." Jekyll assures her as he sat and hung his head in shame.
"Hey, shhhh, I know" She went over and stood very close to him, her perfume again intoxicating him. Jekyll stayed sat down as she positioned herself almost between his legs. "Listen, I think we stand a really good chance of a beautiful and long lasting friendship, maybe more, but we have to forget about what's happened and focus on the future Dr Jekyll."
"Thank you doctor, I would like that." He looks up at her as they gaze into each others eyes, very close at this point. Dr Jekyll is unsure what she she wants, but he knows what he wants. She suddenly backs off a couple of paces "I er, need to head off, I'm meeting a friend for lunch."

She made her excuses, perhaps thinking she was rushing into things.

"Sure, sorry to keep you. Pop round soon though yeah."

"Will do, say hi to Hyde for me."

Jekyll smiles. "He's says hi back. Go on go, I don't want to make you late" he tells her as she's meandering towards the door. He follows her and locks it afterwards. He can't help but think how perfect life could be with her. She clearly felt the same way - time is needed.

CHAPTER NINE

LET'S GO HUNTING

Knowing she was still out there was eating Hyde up. He couldn't contain himself. But how do we go about finding her. She could be anywhere by now. Jekyll tried to keep him calm but it wasn't working. The relationship was getting strained again. They sat in their dining room doing nothing but battling thoughts against each other. They obsessed about it over and over again but couldn't think of how to find someone who doesn't want to be caught. They had exhausted Dr Jekylls limited computer knowledge, but maybe Jinny Wu wasn't even her real name. Hyde suggests going to the casino to try and get some clues. Jekyll reluctantly agrees.

The casino was almost empty, a clear sign that Jinny Wu was no longer around. He clients and cronies have cleared out pending the police investigation, as it goes, this is probably the safest place for them to be right now. Would she come back for revenge, would she try and get to them? Maybe she would just disappear into the sunset. The guns that were confiscated must have cost a fortune but human lives are priceless. How can someone be that callous? "She has to pay" Hyde repeatedly told Dr Jekyll. Jekyll knew that Hyde would eventually get his own way, so he may as well try and help. They sat at a poker table and started a few hands with no sign of anyone or anything suspicious. There is a chap behind them playing black jack who has a few stitches on his head from a cut, Jekyll nor Hyde can tell if its one of the thugs they took down so they kept playing, but keeping their wits about them. No drinks brought over this time Jekyll noticed. No nice service like he used to get. He wondered if she was just watching him as they played. But nothing. Jekyll noticed the door to her office was unmanned, never before was it unmanned. He decided to go for it as not many people were around. He got to the door and twisted the gold door knob to the left and to his surprise it opened. The room was empty. An old ruffled red carpet on the floor with some engrained markings on it where Jinny's desk once sat. Some wires sticking out of the wall where her CCTV was once kept. Someone has ripped everything out in a hurry. It smelt of mould and no heating was on. There was nothing to be gained by snooping further. Jekyll left.

By the end of the night they were very frustrated and a little drunk. Jekyll walked by the shipyard as they left and the crime scene was still taped off. No chance of her being there. They decided to go home via the corner shop which was (thankfully) back up and running for Dr Jekyll to get his drink.
"Ah Dr Jekyll, my favourite superhero" Sam said as entered.
"HA, I am no superhero Sam" He graciously turns down the praise. "I am though" Hyde told Jekyll.
He went to the back of the store and chose a bottle of whiskey, his usual of course.
"You won't believe this Sam, I am out of cigarettes, I'll take 20" He surprises the shopkeeper with his request.
"Ah Dr Jekyll, I knew this day would finally come." Sam told Jekyll, very pleased with himself. With all the excitement of the last few days Dr Jekyll had forgot to order his usual shipment from overseas. He returned to the counter put his whiskey down to pay while Sam slammed some cigarettes down for him. "You don't pay here Dr" Sam told Jekyll again.

"Come on Sam, take my money" Jekyll pleaded.
"No sir." Your money is no good here." off you go.
"You're a good man Sam" he tells him as he walks out and heads home.

They get home and decide to turn in for the night. Another day passed without being able to find Wu. Hyde grew more and more impatient. He didn't want revenge, he just didn't want her to do this to any other kids. Jekyll was a bit more vengeful perhaps, he wanted to make her pay for what she had done. As he laid there in bed with a lamp on in the corner and the blinds fully drawn his attention turned to the doctor. He hasn't heard from her in a few days. I should call her tomorrow he thinks. Yes you should thinks Hyde.

The next morning Jekyll fells exhausted for the first time in a long time. He felt like he had been hit by a bus. "Hyde, what did you do?" he said out loud.
"She can't be allowed to get away with it" Hyde told him. His legs ached, cramp in his calfs. He tries to stretch it out.
"What did you do?"
"I went hunting." Hyde told him.

"Any luck?" Jekyll's interest peaked.
"No luck" he says in an usually sad voice.
"You didn't?"
"Didn't what?"
"You know?"
"No, what?" A strange back and forth occurs between one man and himself.
"Cause any.... damage? Jekyll tried to be delicate in accusing his largely unstable psychopathic alter ego of slaughtering people.
"What do you take me for? I only ever get into trouble because of you or from trying to help people!" Hyde retaliates in anger. "I know, I'm sorry. I just had to check"

Jekyll has some breakfast and a couple of coffees to get himself going. It hit him like a bullet of energy after not being dependant on them recently. He suddenly felt alive and raring to go. He picked up his phone and called the Doctor. They hadn't heard from her in a little while and he thought they were growing closer. It went straight to voicemail which was unusual for her, but maybe she was relaxing, maybe she was on holiday for all he knew! He would pop round later in the day to check on her.

He popped into the shop and exchanged the usual pleasantry's with Sam and returned home to catch up on the headlines. He saves the crossword for later in the day. He liked something to look forward to. It got to around 3pm and Jekyll tried the doctor again, still her phone was off. He wanted to go and check on her, but didn't want to look desperate. Sod it, they're friends! Why not! So he heads off to her apartment building. He didn't know the flat she lived in but he did know the building. He went to the buzzers and saw Peterson on one of the buzzers. He buzzed the buzzer and loud shrill noise came out of the speaker. There was no answer after ten seconds so he buzzed it again. Number 14 was not responding. "Something is wrong" Hyde whispers to him. Someone came up behind Jekyll and opened the door with their key. "Thank you, I can't seem to find my key" Hyde jumped in before Jekyll could say anything and they made there way up to flat 14. He knocked on the door and waited patiently. The corridor was immaculately kept with glass balustrades and a perfectly perpendicular doormat outside. Jekyll checked under it for a key, nothing. A plant pot with a small fern stood next to the door. Still no key. Maybe people don't leave a spare key out anymore like they used to. He banged on the door again. There was no answer. Now Jekyll was worried. He went home again to think about his next steps. Through the park and into his road when he notices a courier bike leaving his house. Another invitation for another charity event no doubt. He took the envelope and sat at the dining room table and looked at the letter he had just received. He hasn't opened it yet, he needs another coffee first. A double espresso from his fancy but noisy coffee machine and then he sits back down again to open the letter. No address on the letter, just two words. Dr Jekyll.

You would expect Dr Jekyll to have a fancy letter opener in the shape of a dagger or something like that, but no, he tears the letter open just like a normal human being. The paper was thick and crisp. He unfolded it and laid it flat on the table.

DR JEKYLL,

IF YOU WANT TO SEE YOUR PRECIOUS DOCTOR FREIND AGAIN YOU WILL COME TO THE SHIP YARD FRIDAY NIGHT 7PM. DOCK NUMBER SIX.

NO POLICE. COME ALONE.

WU.

It was written in all capitals and no doubt that it was Jinny Wu. Hyde instantly stood up and flipped the table over in anger. He turned and smashed things off the side table. Jekyll couldn't control him as he yelled in anger. "We take her down now" Hyde insists. "Look, we know where she will be and when she will be there. We can save her." Jekyll promises. Friday was two days away. Hyde had no choice but to wait. It was infuriating. Two days of drinking whiskey and plotting how we was going to make Jinny Wu pay for this - Hyde had pretty much taken over. He hadn't realised just how fond he had become of the doctor.

Friday came, not quickly enough. Dr Jekyll was back in control and they were going to do exactly what Jinny Wu wanted. He was sure that it would all be ok.

CHAPTER TEN

LET HER GO

As per the message they got from Jinny Wu they set out to find the ship that had the Doctor on board. It was a very calm and quiet ship yard and not a cloud in the sky, the moon and stars reflected off the tranquil sea. Jekyll and Hyde walk up the galley of a ship in the docks, they enter the deck at the bow, weaving through the crates and storage boxes slowly and deliberately. They go down some steel steps and into the belly of the ship into an opening. There stands Jinny with several of her thugs and the doctor in restraints.

Jinny...we have you, let the doctor go." shouts Jekyll.
"We?" Jinny laughs and looks at her thugs "I think your army have ran away Dr Jekyll. It's just you"
"Dr Jekyll...please tell me Hyde is with you." begged the doctor.
"Are we expecting friends? I didn't think you had any friends Jekyll." Jinny Wu still enjoying herself at this

point, the thugs keeping a close eye out for any sign of an ambush.

"We do not need friends..." Hyde says with a look of revenge in his eyes. He is ready to rip her limb from limb. Hyde can feel Jekyll holding him back. '"Let's kill this fucking psycho, stop holding me back." Hyde demands.

"No...we need to take her in" argues Jekyll. "She needs to pay by the letter of the law." Hyde shows his frustration by grinding his teeth and pacing. Jinny Wu is utterly baffled. "Are you ok Dr? Are you cracking up?" she chuckles to her thugs around her, all of whom are getting itchy trigger fingers while this talk carries on.

"We're not taking her in, this ends now, I'm gonna rip her fucking face off" Hyde shouts.

"You are delusional Jekyll, need some more of your serum...? get him boys" She orders her men and they converge on Jekyll. One giant man of a thug and Jinny stay, holding doctor and her rope bound wrists.

One of the thugs run towards Jekyll wielding a machete above his head, ready to hack Jekyll in half. Hyde hits the thug, with an uppercut like thunder, lifting him off the ground and flying back into another thug as two more run in to join the fight. Hyde grapples with the thugs, one jumps on his back and hangs on with his arms around Hyde's neck while the other proceeds to punch Hyde in the stomach. The punches hit hard but Hyde can't help but laugh at the guy punching him. They really are having no impact on him at all "You'll have to do better than that" He tells him. He grabs the thug on his back by his head and pulling him forward over his shoulder, he throws him at the thug in front of him and they fall over like a couple of dominos and are rendered unconscious. The third thug frantically flails a knife in front of Hyde's face, Hyde grabs the thug's arm, nearly pulling it off, he spins the thug around, throwing him into the wall of the ship with all mighty clang of his head hitting the metal.

Hyde turns his hyped up attention to Jinny Wu. She is understandably shaking and scared at what she as just witnessed. "I suggest you get her go" Hyde says stalking toward Jinny. She puts her dagger to the doctors throat. "Don't come any closer" she warns as she holds it against the doctors neck.
"I don't want to kill you Jinny." Jekyll insists
"I do" Hyde intervenes.

"We are going to do the right thing and turn you in to the police" Jekyll promises. During this little chat with himself he was edging closer to the doctor and Jinny, but Jinny was so pre occupied with the bizarre altercation that she didn't notice him creeping forward. Suddenly he flings himself at Jinny, grabbing her wrist so she drops the knife and falls to the floor with Jekyll on top of her. Just then a loud metal clad ringing sounds throughout the ship, and another...Bang! Jekyll knew he had been shot, he felt the moist hole in his clothing. "What the fuck?" he turned around and saw the man, semi conscious on the floor pointing the gun in his general direction. He gets another round off but it goes nowhere near. Hyde walks over to the man and grabs him by the throat and holds it until there is no longer any air leaving his body and he lay motionless. He turned his attentions back to Jinny Wu. Looking at her like a lion who has just found his prey for the night.
"Let's take care of her now" Hyde says.
"No, we can't, we have spoken about this" Jekyll responds.
"Fuck that, she deserves it" Hyde tells the doctor who is thinking about the ramifications more than Hyde. He stalks towards Jinny, blood soaking through his clothes but doesn't seem to be causing him any issues. He picks her up by the throat, hoisting her feet off the

floor and looking at her in the eyes as she choked trying to wriggle away. Her face turning purple as he did. "Hyde, this is wrong, stop!" Jekyll pleaded with him.
Hyde remained undeterred as he held here there, her flailing becoming less and less.

The doctor approaches Hyde and put her hand on his arm in a soft caring way. "Hyde, you need to let her go. She will pay more if we hand her over to the police. A lifetime trapped in a small room with no escape Mr Hyde. You know how that feels, how lonely that is..." Hyde thinks for a moment before letting her down and collapsing, Jinny gasping for air, falls to the floor and is rendered helpless while the doctor uses the ropes to tie her up. She turns her attention to Jekyll who is now on the floor pressing a cloth against his wound trying to stem the blood. The doctor calls an ambulance before helping him put pressure on the bloodstained clothes where the wound is. "You'll be fine" she promises Jekyll.
"If we die, you need to make sure people know the truth. We did good here"

"What the fuck are you? You freak!" Jinny Wu listening to a the conversation. "We? What's this we you crazy son of a bitch?" she carries on.
"Shut the fuck up" the doctor screams at her before walking over to her and striking her across the face. The doctor turned around and heard the sirens in the distance.
"You're gonna be fine, the ambulance is here" the doctor reassured Jekyll. But he did not respond. The doctor just cradled him.

The police burst in to the ship first, followed by the medics. They were just silhouettes of flashing blue lights against the night sky. They see Jekyll laying on the floor in a puddle of blood being held by the doctor. Jinny Wu tied up, beaten up and motionless. A chair collapsed on the floor. The medics rush over to the blood stricken Dr Jekyll and usher the doctor away and start tending to him. A police officer puts a foil blanket around the doctor and accompanies her out of the tanker and into the view of the police chief who had just arrived and got out of his car. He wasn't wearing a suit, he had clearly been woken up and dragged onto the crime scene.
"Doctor, are you ok?" He stupidly asks.

"No chief, its been a horrid ordeal" as she looks around at the surrounding area being taped off and lights erected, it was like a military operation.
He takes her over to the ambulance to get her checked out. "What on earth happened here?" he asks here in a confused tone. She watches on as the police busy themselves.
"Please just make sure that Dr Jekyll is ok?" she tears up as she makes the request. The chief puts his arm round her and holds her close with a few comforting words, none of which the doctor really hears. She saw through her teary eyes Jinny Wu being escorted out of the ship and into a police car.

Her tears seem to dry up as the anger takes over when she looks at her. "She needs to pay." the doctor says "You will make sure she pays wont you" she asks of the chief.
"What did she do? What went on here?" he is still confused by the whole thing.
"It's hard to…" She started but saw Jekyll being wheeled out on a stretcher. She gets up and runs over to see him. He has three paramedics around him and a blanket to keep him warm. The trolly trundles slowly over the uneven ground as she gets closer and grabs

his hand "Will he be ok?" she asks as they continue to move toward the ambulance. She clings on to his hand without anything in return. She fears the worst. Jekyll is loaded into the back of the ambulance as her grip is broken. She watches on as the ambulance doors are shut and it drives off with the sirens blaring as her eyes start to fill up again. She is stood statuesque with tears running down her face, everything seemed muted and in slow-motion. She had no feeling at all. Numb. She felt the chief's arm come around her again. "Doctor, come on, we need to get you to the station. I know it's difficult, but we have to talk about what happened."
"No, I want to go to the hospital." The doctor resists.
"We can go there afterwards, I promise." He assures her. She turned and looks him dead in the eye through her water laden eyes and told him "I am going to the hospital. You can take me, or I will make my own way there." The chief didn't want to upset her anymore than she clearly already was, she might just clam up fully on what happened, so he decided to indulge her.
"Of course, I will take you. Come on" He ushers her toward his car and they make their way to the hospital.

The hospital is only a 25 minute drive, but it already felt like forever since they left the crime scene. "They won't allow you to see him straight away, you know that don't you?" the police chief told her only to be met with a stony silence. The doctors eyes fixated on the passing lights as they drove along the road, the occasional glance at a bus stop or petrol station ruining the constant stream to street lights. "He will probably be in surgery, or recovery." The chief continues. The doctor closes her eyes and another tears rolls down her cheek as she does. She thought she might have ran out of tears by now. The chief looks over and sees she is asleep, she probably needs the rest.

CHAPTER ELEVEN

YOU'RE A LUCKY MAN

The anxious doctor is sat with the exhausted looking police chief. They are sat on small red plastic chairs which are very uncomfortable and the only colour in the plain looking corridors. Why did they make hospitals so boring? Surely, if there's one place you want to be cheered up with bright and vibrant colours - it's a hospital! The pair are talking, of course, about Dr Jekyll. The doctor was very conscious that these secrets are not hers to tell, and Dr Jekyll and Mr Hyde had just saved her life. She owed them a huge debt of gratitude, the least she could do is to make sure the police (or anyone) doesn't know what went on until Dr Jekyll is ready to tell them.
"I'm sure Jekyll will be alright, he is a strong man." The police chief was trying to reassure the doctor. "stubborn too, so I don't see him going anywhere soon." went on the chief wearily as he looked at his watch. He's been at work for almost 20 hours today he

noticed. His wife is very understanding, but this is pushing boundaries even by their standards.

The worried doctor become visibly upset about the state of her new found hero, a shadow of doubt slowly creeping across her pale face.

"I pray you are right chief, I don't understand what possessed them to run into a bullet, they are so gung-ho sometimes."

"They?" The police chief notices her slip.

"Pardon?" The doctor realises her mistake and tries to buy to some time.

"You said they are so gung-ho, was there someone else there?" The chief said, full of suspicions, now leaning forward on the plastic chair, creaking as he did so.

"Er...no...no there wasn't, I'm still a little shook up and not thinking straight at the moment." she lied and she forced out some crocodile tears for the chief's benefit. Leaning forward to match him and putting her head in her hands.

"Yes, that's understandable under the circumstances." the police chief puts his hand on the doctor's shoulder, who still has her head down, visibly upset for the chief's benefit.

"We will have to do this formally, but can you tell me what happened, please...take your time." the sympathetic voice of the chief ringing throughout the corridor.

It was still very quiet in this part of the hospital. Perhaps they closed it to the public given the circumstances or maybe its just a quiet night thought the doctor, begging for someone to interrupt them so they might just put an end to this conversation and go and check on Dr Jekyll and Mr Hyde.

She wiped her nose on her sleeve leaving two snotty white streaks on the plain black hoody. She nodded her head.
"Some of it is a little fuzzy, but I will do my best" she assured the chief as she pondered which details she could get away with leaving out.
"Anything you can remember is valuable information," he pleaded.
"Well I was approaching my apartment when a car pulled up along side me and asked me for the time."
"Do you know what type of car?"

"Chief" she giggled "I don't know my ford from my fiat at the best of times" she said.
"That's ok." He reassured her. "Carry on"
"They bundled me into the boot and took my phone. We then drove for maybe 45 minutes? Then they got me out, we were at the shipyard."
"KIDNAPPED!" he croaked, shaking his head.
"Yes, kidnapped...by Jinny Wu"
"Jinny Wu?" he murmured
"Yes, she kidnapped me because she knew Dr Jekyll and I were close, I think she wanted to use me to get to Dr Jekyll,"
"Why would she want to get to Dr Jekyll?" quizzed the chief.
"To kill him, and it looks like she might have succeeded."
"Its all under control, you don't need to worry about that now doctor." he told her in a comforting way.
"Please continue doctor," he urged.
"Jinny wants Jekyll out of the way, Jekyll found about about some rather unscrupulous businesses she is involved in." she went on to explain to the chief. In all this time, still no one had come along the corridor which the doctor thought was strange, only another two police officers on some benches a few meters along.
"Is this area open to the public?" asked the doctor.

"No ma'am. When there's a situation like this we tend to secure a small area of the hospital.
"She runs some businesses... " She thinks how to explain it. "It's people trafficking, drug smuggling and illegal gambling racket" She reels the off counting them on her fingers for maximum effect for the chief.

The police chief at this point stood up and stepped away, very shocked. "W...what!...I don't believe it, Jinny is the backbone of the community" he stutters in disbelief.
Upon overhearing the conversation a police officer stood nearby steps over and talks to the chief. It was the same skinny chap who interviewed Dr Jekyll after the previous incident. "Erm excuse me chief, sorry to interrupt" he does so anyway. "Yes...what is it?" he was exasperated at this point. "The doctor might be onto something chief, a few months back we had Dr Jekyll in after another altercation at the ship yard. We took a statement from him about Miss Jinny Wu." The police chief was a bit baffled "Why did I not know about this, well what did he say?"
"He said that Jinny Wu was the leader of a people and drug smuggling ring and was a murderer, we thought

Hyde had been drinking again and thought nothing of it"

"It's hard to believe myself, Jinny has been a great service to this community. Thank you officer." The police man walks away while the chief and the doctor continue their conversation.

"Well doctor, we have her in custody so we can question her" the chief confirmed.

"That's why she wanted Jekyll dead, I am sure of it, he knows everything about her operation." The doctor doubled down.

At that moment the doors to the operating theatre swung open and an unconscious Dr Jekyll was being wheeled out on a big bed with wheels and a drip attached above his head. Three doctors and nurses around him. They were all dressed in scrubs as if they had just finished with Dr Jekyll. The doctor has no idea what to think. Would they wheel a dead man through the corridor, if he was ok, why is he not awake? They both sprung up immediately and walked towards the bed being wheeled along. The surgeon breaks away from the others and comes to head off the doctor and chief "He will be fine, he just needs some rest" stated the surgeon. The doctor collapses back into a sitting position onto a seat behind her still clutching the foil blanket around her for warmth and comfort.

A few hours later Jekyll is laying in his bed, propped up halfway and awake. The room has some partly drawn blinds and a TV in it, which Jekyll would not be at all interested in, although he intended to spend no time here at all.

The Doctor taps on the door and opens it "Dr Jekyll, the surgeon said I could pop in and see you?" no longer sporting the tin foil.
"Of course, come in" He tells her shuffling up the bed to be a tiny bit more upright.
"How are you feeling? she asked suddenly thinking its probably a very stupid question.
"Like I have been shot Doctor." He responds with a modicum of humour.
"Sorry, stupid question"
"Honestly, don't be silly. Thank you for asking. I am fine, I think. Bullet removed and all stitched up. I think Hyde's strength stopped any real damage."

"Well then I guess we have to be thankful to Mr Hyde."
"Hmmmm" Dr Jekyll solemnly responded.
"What's wrong?" the doctor sensing his tone.
"I haven't felt him since" Jekyll admits in a quiet voice incase anyone overhears.
"You are a very lucky man Dr Jekyll" He hears as the door opens. The police chief has come to see if the hero of the hour is recovering ok.
"To be alive chief, I know. It's a miracle sir, and thank you for looking after me." He likes to feed the ego of the authorities in the hope that they will be on his side if things ever get out in the open.
"Well, yes and to have the doctor by your side." The chief notices that the Doctor is clasping Jekyll's hand with both of hers. Jekyll stares up at her and smiles a deep smile. "Yes...yes I am, she is quite remarkable isn't she." he concedes.

There's another tap at the door as the surgeon pokes his head in. "It's like piccadilly circus in here today, I just want some peace and quiet" Hyde tells Jekyll internally. Jekyll can't help smiling. The surgeon looking up from Jekyll's notes in his hand "You really are lucky to be here Mr Jekyll, by all accounts you should be dead, and you're sat here smiling like a cheshire chat" The surgeon tells him noticing the smirk on his face.

"Thank you, just happy to be alive." Happy to hear from Hyde more like. He spent most of his life trying to suppress him, now it looks as though they are inseparable again.

"The speed of your recovery is unheard of, we would like to take some blood and run some tests please Dr Jekyll." Jekyll felt the doctors hands tighten around his hand as he tried to think of an excuse.

"Sir!" a young doctor burst in through the door "We need you in triage now please" and he leaves as quickly as he came.

"I'll send a nurse in later to take those bloods. All being well you should be able to be discharged tomorrow." He explains to Jekyll before he leaves the room.

"We can't have those tests" Hyde tells Jekyll the obvious. Whatever would it show? Jekyll was curious in all honesty but he knew it would raise far too many questions.

Hyde was right. They have to get out before they come back to take those bloods, but without raising suspicion.
"Yes, Jekyll it is remarkable, whats..."
"Chief, Jekyll can tell you more about Jinny Wu"
"Ah...yes...Jinny Wu" Jekyll said catching on to the doctors clever distraction. "Where do I start" he begins.
He proceeds to explain to the doctor what had happened in pretty much the same level of detail that the Doctor had explained. They didn't have long before the ambulance and police arrived on the ship but they did get their story straight before the flashing lights drew in. As the doctor pushed down on the wound to try and stem the bleeding, they agreed would make sure Jinny Wu went down for a long time without letting anyone find out about Mr Hyde.

"The last thing I remember is running toward Jinny on the ship, to try and save the good doctor here, then I wake up here." Jekyll finished the lie and didn't give the chief much to go on.
"Ok Dr. Jekyll, thank you, we will go to this club of hers and the docks. We will be having a talk with Miss Wu" the chief smiles at Jekyll and the doctor, before

turning away and opening the door, he turns back and tell Dr Jekyll "Goodbye doctors. No more running into bullets yeah" He leaves and closes the door behind him leaving them alone once more. "Well it looks like Jinny will finally get what she deserves" Jekyll tells the doctor - and himself.

"Yes, thanks to both of you...Hyde" she remembers Jekyll hadn't felt him since the shooting.

"Yes, I'm here my dear, did you miss me...I was welling up when I saw how worried you were about us when we got shot." Hyde laughed as he finally showed himself in public again.

"You mean you were there the whole time?" the doctor asked him.

"Yes, of course I have been...what did you expect me to introduce myself to the chief and all of his little solders" Hyde told her.

"Well...no...no I didn't, but you could have given me a sign"

"So you were worried about us then doctor?" he probed further.

"Maybe" she said bashfully. "Come on, lets get you out of here before the nurse starts sticking needles in you. She helps him up and into a wheelchair. She pops a blanket over him and tucks a blue blanket over his legs and tucks it in. She goes and pokes her head out of the door and its just as quiet as before. She sneaks him out and along the corridor. It was still deathly quiet in the hospital and they made their way to the nearest exit. Who'd have thought the fire escape drawings would actually come in useful the doctor thought. They got themselves into the car park and the doctor helped Jekyll into her car. She drove to his place and got him laid up on the sofa. "I'll make you a tea" she told him as she made her way to the kitchen.

Jinny Wu sat in the police interview room. It was bright, lit up by several lights in the ceiling. A singular desk with three chairs around it and a door locked by a key pad with numbers on it. She had declined the offer of a lawyer. She looked exhausted, probably up all night thinking about what the outcome would be. Revenge on Dr Jekyll perhaps? She feels a cold sweat come over her as the police chief and another officer walk in. "Miss Wu" the chief makes his presence known as he and his colleague sit down. "It seems we have a lot to discuss." Opening a file and shuffling papers around. She is visibly shaken and knows that she doesn't have a leg to stand on. "No comment." She says in her usual shrill tone.

"Well, we need to know Miss Wu, are you working for someone or are you working alone?"
"My English has taken a turn for the worse, I can't really understand"
"Be smart here Jinny, you can cut a deal" He tries to get her on side.

"Ha. You think there's a deal to be done?" She says suddenly a little more annoyed with the situation.
"There must be something you can give us Miss Wu, otherwise we have to assume that you were the head of this entire operation. The guns, the children, the trafficking, the drugs. That's a lot of jail time right there." The police chief trying to convince her to give him something to go on.

She looks at the ground and takes a long pause as if to think very carefully about her response. "Then I guess you will have to assume whatever you see fit" She responds coldly.
"Then I guess the interview is over" he tells her as he stands up and grabs his jacket off the back of the chair.

The other officer takes his lead and walks to the door and opens it.
"Please tell Dr Jekyll to visit me in prison." She asks of the police chief. He looks at her blankly, why would she want that? He ponders a response but doesn't bother. They leave the room, leaving Jinny Wu to her own thoughts.

CHAPTER TWELVE

YOU HAVE NO IDEA

You're a very lucky man Dr Jekyll, the words of the police chief still ringing in his ears as he sat on the sofa. It was a quiet sunny afternoon as he lay there watching the trees sway in the summer breeze. No noise, just him, his thoughts... and Mr Hyde. It felt like they were finally at peace. Jinny Wu in the hands of the law. He had everything laid out next to him thanks to the good doctor. A drink and some snacks, a crossword book and the TV remote, not that he would use that. The doctor was coming by later with the daily papers. He wasn't drinking whiskey due to the painkillers which was a refreshing change for them. His wound healing nicely, but still relying upon the doctor the change his dressings for him on a regular basis. He should be pretty much independent by now, but he is enjoying the attention of the doctor playing nurse. The house now had a few house plants arounds the place. The doctor assures Jekyll they will help with the recovery.

The doctor soon returned with his daily papers. He still liked to be kept abreast of the local news and was waiting to hear about Jinny Wu being charged. She came through the door and shouted "Morning"
"Morning" said Jekyll.
"Morning" said Hyde.
It wasn't even weird for her any more. She had become accustomed to it. They sat chatting for a while before it was time to change his dressing again. This would probably be the last time it needs changing.

Over the last week while laying around not being able to go out, Jekyll put his time and money to good use. He set up a charity for refugees and people who needed protection from the likes of Jinny Wu. It was widely publicised and he has been asked to make some speeches or give some interviews, but he has declined. The headlines have stopped about this for now, but they will return he is sure.

He picked up the papers in search of the headlines he had longed for but nothing was there again. The chief had popped round during his recovery to check in on Jekyll and to let him know that she would be going away for a long time, but he wanted to see if it made the papers. He folded the paper up an threw it on the floor just as the doctor came in with a fresh cup of tea for him. "Did you see it?" the doctor asked. "Nothing in there about Wu" he said disappointed.
"No, but did you read at the bottom of the first page?" the doctor pointed out. He strained as he picked up the paper again. He huffed and puffed as he read the dull and boring headlines. He reads the one he thinks she is on about "Crime Does Pay" it reads, an ex convict is throwing a gala in order to raise money for under privileged children. There is a widespread theory that the money he has still comes from a large crime syndicate.

"Have you not had enough excitement?" He asks the doctor.
"I think this is why you have theses abilities Dr Jekyll, to help people who need it and to stop people like this.
"You think we should attend the gala?"
"I think you should make an appearance. It may be the perfect opportunity to make a speech about your charity." she suggests.
"I will need a clean suit." Jekyll hints
"Already at the dry cleaners." she tells him
"Ah. I'll also need a date." He drops a bigger hint.
"My favourite dress is also in the dry cleaners" She has it all planned already. She walks out of the sitting room to make a cup of tea.

The gala is a wash with people in ball gowns and tuxedos as people mingled and networked. Most of them there to serve their own selfish purpose of elevating their status or public perception of themselves, but it all raises money for charity so Dr Jekyll was on board. He felt ten feet tall as he walked in with the doctor on his arm. She was wearing a long navy blue tight dress and her long blonde hair curled and draped over her slender shoulders. The ballroom was beautifully done out and TV camera's were rolling.

There was a huge crystal chandelier hanging above the centre of the room with a hardwood dance floor and a bar in the corner. Dr Jekyll felt nervous. When he asked for a ticket to the event they asked him if he would mind doing a speech as his charity is pretty well intertwined with the one the ball is raising money for. He reluctantly agreed to do so and the doctor said she would obviously give him the emotional support he needed.

The police chief came over and spoke to the pair of them (Or all three of them depending who you speak to)
"Nice to see you back on your feet Dr Jekyll" the chief said.
"Thank you sir" He shakes him by his outstretched hand and smiles at him.
"Doctor, nice to see you again." the police chief continues his pleasantries. She shakes his hand and smiles.
 "Any news on Jinny Wu being convicted?" Jekyll quizzed the police chief.
"The sentencing is next week, you wont need to worry about her again" the chief reassured him.
"Thank you" He said.

"This is a nice gig isn't it?" The police chief changes the subject as he looks around at the band playing and the people chatting in their little cliques.
"If you like that kind of thing" he bats back
"Oh, I am looking forward to your speech Dr Jekyll, the cameras will be on, so don't fuck it up" he looks deadly serious for a couple of seconds and then his face cracks when he laughs out loud "Only kidding, you'll be fine." he pats him on the shoulder and walks away.
"Ha! Thanks Chief" he tries to join in the fun.
"Funny prick ain't he" Hyde couldn't help it.

They continue towards the bar hoping not to get stopped by anyone else until they have at least two to three whiskeys inside them. They grab their drinks and look around at the people they are surrounded by, never have they felt more out of place with Hyde not suppressed. It still crosses Dr Jekylls mind, what if someone really upset Hyde and he came out, he flips and throws someone out of a window. Hyde assures him there is nothing to worry about on a regular basis.
"Are you ready Dr Jekyll?" a voice comes out of nowhere. It's one of the organisers. Jekyll snaps out of his own thoughts and looks at the doctor. She gives him a warm and reassuring smile and a squeeze of his

hand. She really does look stunning Hyde reminds him. He looks back at the organiser and tells her he's ready. He makes his way towards the stage with the organiser speaking to him as they went. He wasn't really listening to her, it didn't matter what she was saying, he knew what he was going to say and who he was keeping an eye out for. Mr Kitari.

Mr Kitari was a nasty piece of work back in the day. He was in prison for eight years on multiple charges. Apparently he bettered himself while he was imprisoned but Dr Jekyll was informed that he was still involved in crime syndicates. Dr Jekyll had not yet had the pleasure to meet Mr Kitari, in fact, he hasn't even seen him at the event. Jekyll approached the side of the stage and was given the signal that he was going to be introduced. The organiser stands up and thanks everyone before saying a few kinds words about Dr Jekyll and his charity. It's only a couple of steps up for Dr Jekyll to get on the stage and stand at the lectern. He isn't used to this anymore, but the butterflies soon disappear as he sees the audience (especially the doctor) smiling back at him. Everyone had heard of his antics so he was a very popular figure in the community all of a sudden.

His speech went down extremely well and he received a rapturous round of applause after finishing his final sentence. On a screen somewhere away from the venue Mr Kitari is watching the ongoing event on the TV. He looks angrily at the TV as the broadcast goes out and accidentally snaps the pencil he was fiddling with at the time. "Dr Jekyll, we should meet..." he says in a very deep menacing voice.

As Dr Jekyll left the stage he was confronted by a news-reporter who wanted a story straight away after the speech.

"Dr Jekyll, thank you for such a heartwarming speech" she said with a huge open mouth smile on her face. Curly brown hair and well dressed with her lanyard on so people could tell she was a journalist. "You referred to WE quite a few times in the speech. The charity only has you listed as the CEO, what you mean by we?" she presses him trying to get information on a silent benefactor maybe.

Dr Jekyll smiles at her and looks past her to the doctor. He looks back at the journalist and thinks for a second.

"You have no idea love" Hyde tells her before walking away and into the congratulatory arms of the doctor. He knew his life from here on in was going to involve using his powers for good. Taking down drug cartels or crime organisations. THey could really do some tangible good in this city if they put their mind to it. They left the event in high spirits and went home to plan the next chapter in their already incredibly complicated life.

ABOUT THE AUTHOR

Dan Brothers is a creator of content from Northampton in England. Born in 1982 he started writing films in his thirties and went on to be an actor and director before publishing his works in book form.

"I love this story. The spin on a classic is always fun to do. Look out for Mr Hyde the feature film coming soon.'"

You can follow Dan on Instagram @dan_stagram13 or twitter @danbrothers13

Special thanks to Pete King who supported the development of the story.

Printed in Great Britain
by Amazon